LEAVING AUTUMN

A SWEET VERMONT HALLOWEEN ROMANCE

SWEET AS MAPLE SYRUP
BOOK ONE

ID JOHNSON

For AnnaClaire. You can do it, girl!

CONTENTS

Chapter 1 — 1
Chapter 2 — 9
Chapter 3 — 17
Chapter 4 — 23
Chapter 5 — 31
Chapter 6 — 39
Chapter 7 — 45
Chapter 8 — 53
Chapter 9 — 61
Chapter 10 — 69
Chapter 11 — 77
Chapter 12 — 85
Chapter 13 — 91
Chapter 14 — 97
Chapter 15 — 105
Chapter 16 — 111
Chapter 17 — 117
Chapter 18 — 123
Chapter 19 — 131
Chapter 20 — 137
Chapter 21 — 143
Chapter 22 — 149
Chapter 23 — 157
Chapter 24 — 163
Chapter 25 — 171
26. Cold Turkey Chapter 1 — 179

Also by ID Johnson — 187

CHAPTER 1

Autumn

My heart! Oh, my heart! I think as I pull out the next seasonal decoration from my Aunt Beverly's newly arrived boxes. It's a set of little ghost figurines with blushing cheeks and cute little eyelashes. One is sporting a bow and a pink Halloween bag, one is holding a twiggy broom with a round black kitten perched at its feet, and the other is holding a neatly carved pumpkin.

This is it. Fall has finally arrived, my favorite time of year, and my namesake will finally be enjoyed to the fullest extent.

"Autumn," my aunt calls from the front of the store. "There's a drawn up plan for the new display here by the register. When you get a chance later, let me know what you think. As you can tell, it's officially time to put out the good Halloween stuff."

I finish placing the cute ghost trio onto the shelf and bound over to the register. For the last couple of weeks, we'd been showcasing all the fall stuff in my aunt's store here in Maple Falls, Vermont. Our townspeople love this time of year because it is the most beautiful place on Earth to experience the vast array of fall's beautiful colors.

The town really comes to life when the mountains shift from green to gold and amber and maple red. Then there's the Autumn Leaves Celebration…. When I was little, I thought it was all for me because of my name.

The door dings and catches my attention. A short and slender older black man pushes the door closed and meets my eyes.

"Mr. Seeley!" I say. I can't contain my excitement. "I wasn't expecting to see you yet!"

He greets me with a warm, bright smile and crinkles in the corners of his aging eyes. "Autumn, you're just the person I was hoping to see."

Randal Seeley is the owner of the tour company that I work for in the fall. For the last five years since I turned twenty, I've been living above my Aunt Bev's antique shop in a little studio apartment. I usually work for her in her store full time, but my heart really feels its fullest when autumn comes around and I get to lead bus tours through Vermont's countryside, showing off the magnificence of our little part of the world at its best time of year. Actually, starting next week, it'll be time to get back to that, which is probably why I'm squeezing Mr. Seeley's hand a little too hard while he greets me.

"What can I do for you, Mr. Seeley?" I ask, finally letting go of his hand and interlacing my fingers in front of me, resting my elbows on the counter.

"Well, Miss Ackerman," he says, with a teasing lilt to his voice, "it's Margie's birthday soon. Coming up here in the next couple of days. I thought this would be the perfect place to find her gift. And the service is quite nice, too," he jests, softly bumping my shoulder with his.

I smile and nod. "Of course. I'd love to help you out. Did you have anything in mind?"

Mr. Seeley fidgets with the collar under his navy blue sweater. "I always get Margie a new piece of jewelry on our anniversary, so, you know, she's got forty years' worth now! For her birthday, I usually take her out of town, but she's not getting around as well right now since her knee replacement, so I think we'll do a nice dinner in and maybe take a drive. I'd like to get her something—a nice gift."

I smile. Oh, how wonderful it must be to share your entire life with someone you love. That's something I've always dreamed of, but it hasn't found me yet. Forty years–I hope I get to make it there with the love of my life someday.

"All right then!" I clap my hands together to bring myself back down the Earth. "You say she's got a lot of jewelry now, but does she have a good way to store it? A couple of weeks ago, we got in this gorgeous jewelry box from the late Victorian era. Would you like to take a look at it?"

Mr. Seeley nods and gives me another genuine smile. "That sounds perfect, actually. I knew I could count on you."

I can't deny the bit of pride that I feel when I help people like this, especially people who have grown to mean so much to me. It just fills my heart like a cozy mug of fresh, warm cider.

I guide Mr. Seeley toward the back of the store where vanity items are located: brushes, makeup related items, jewelry, and, yes, jewelry boxes. I place my hand on top of one of the gorgeous new one we've just acquired. Besides the gold engravings in the cherry wood finish, it has several other features she may like, such as small drawers, a special place for rings, and a removable board with holes for earrings.

"It opens on both sides and can hold twenty-two necklaces," I explain, demonstrating. "If you don't like this one, we have a few others to choose from, but this particular one has a lovely blush colored velvet lining. I recall Mrs. Seeley wearing pink quite often, so maybe she'd enjoy this color. And the finish is amazing. It's held up well over the years."

Mr. Seeley inspects the drawers by pulling them out and opening the little doors on the sides. He presses the carousel for the necklaces and seems pleased that it turns. "This is quite nice," he agrees. "I think I'll take it."

"Great!" I say. "I hope she loves it."

"Could you wrap it up for me?"

I nod and carefully carry it to the register. It's not too heavy, but it has enough weight to it that I hope it's easy for him to get it home to his wife I'm sure she can find a nice place for it in their lovely home. I take out a box from beneath the counter and carefully pack it inside.

As I'm sizing up the box for how much wrapping paper I'll need, Mr. Seeley sparks up a conversation.

"I know you love autumn more than anything, Autumn," he says. "But how was your summer? I don't usually see you often this time of year."

I tell him a bit about how I joined my parents on one of their RV trips over to Maine, soaked up a bit of sun in my friend's pool, worked at the shop, and read. "Summer is just a bit too hot for me," I explain. "I like to stay indoors until fall. I prefer cuddling up in a blanket and sweater when things cool off."

Mr. Seeley chuckles. "And do you have anyone to cuddle up with now?"

His question catches me off guard, and my face flushes immediately. "Mr. Seeley," I groan, feeling the blush in my cheeks and staring down at the tape, hoping he doesn't notice. "You know how hard it is to find people in our small town. I love this place and I want to stay here forever, but I haven't met anyone new in quite some time."

Mr. Seeley nods. "I get it. Margie and I were childhood friends. We were in our twenties before I started seeing her that way. And after I realized I was in love with her, it took a lot of convincing to get her to date me." He laughs to himself and looks up toward the ceiling as if he can see their life playing out up there. "That time will come when you least expect it, and maybe from a place you hadn't realized."

His sincerity helps me to relax, and I feel my cheeks slowly return to normal. I'm not sure what to say, so I just nod and ask him which bow he'd like me to use. He chooses pink, of course.

"Are you ready for the fall touring season?" Mr. Seeley asks as I finish up curling the tendrils of the bow.

I nod excitedly. Next Monday is the official kickoff of the seasonal tours, and for the first week, I get to show off the town's apple orchard and some of the scenic rolling hills. Summer always seems to weigh me down and make everything feel heavy, but when autumn comes and the air gets cooler and lighter, and the trees release from the struggle of retaining water and perk up–when the greens give way to the vibrant yellows, oranges, and reds–that's when the world feels right. It only lasts for a couple of months, but that's another thing that makes it so sweet. In that magical, fleeting time between the oppressive heat and the bone-rattling cold, everything is perfect.

"I'm so looking forward to it," I say.

Mr. Seeley pays for the gift, and I help carry it out to his car. We part ways with a simple wave and smile, and I'm left feeling even more impassioned about starting these tours and experiencing all of my favorite things again.

When I walk back into my aunt's store, she's leaning against the shelves staring at me with a longing expression.

"What?" I ask. "Why does your face look like that?"

Aunt Bev dramatically sniffles and runs over to me, squeezing me against her body like a long-lost child. She rubs her cheek against mine like she used to when I was a teenager and she was purposefully trying to annoy me. "I'm gonna miss you so much!" she whimpers.

I try not to chuckle and let her continue to love on me. "It's not like you'll never see me again. I live upstairs, you know. Plus, I'll still be working here some evenings."

Aunt Bev lets out a hefty sigh and releases all of me but my wrist, which she holds gingerly. "I know that, dear, but you'll be so busy with your tours and all the events around town that ten or so hours feels like a pinch of flavorless salt."

I cock my head at her and press my lips together to keep myself from smiling. She is so dramatic when it comes to the people she loves. While outsiders often see her as a tough-as-nails independent woman, those who are close to her, like me and my mother, know she is actually as soft as putty.

Putting my hands on her shoulders and looking her square in the eye, I tell her, "I won't forget to hang out with you. I promise."

She gives another lofty sigh and goes back to organizing her shelf display. "I know you love fall the most, but what were your favorite things about summer this year?" she asks over her shoulder.

I accompany her and study the display image she's drawn out. "The usual stuff. Cally invited me over to her parents' house to swim pretty often, so that was nice. And of course our Fourth of July festivities were memorable, as always." I chuckle at the thought of the grocer, Mr. Farris, chasing down my puppy Tess, who had stolen a whole package of unopened hotdogs at the picnic, and his nine-year-old son accidentally dropping a firework and sending shots of colored fire into a nearby open garage. Luckily, nobody was hurt, and we all just laughed it off. "I finished several more books, and I was able to finish some more fall festival decorations early. I have some good ideas for this year's—"

Suddenly, the door dings again, and a familiar short, thin-framed girl with jet black shoulder-length hair walks in. She removes her dramatic red cat-eye glasses that look straight out of the '50s to reveal her piercing blue eyes.

"Cally Stein!" my aunt yells. "How could you let Autumn waste another summer the same way she always does! You're my only hope in getting her to socialize with boys so she can stop reading romance books and start living one!"

Cally just shrugs and puts her sunglasses on top of her head. "The problem isn't necessarily that she isn't going out. It's that when she goes out, she doesn't make the effort to talk to new people."

I glare at my best friend. How could she betray me like this? "I talk to people all day long, especially on my tours. It's not my fault that guys don't talk to me!"

Aunt Bev shakes her head and clicks her tongue.

"And why are you both ganging up on me as soon as she walks in the door? I thought you loved me," I complain, crossing my arms.

"Baby girl," Cally says flatly. "We both love you. That's why we tease you."

I purse my lips. I know it's all in good fun, but really, this is an issue I'm a little insecure about. I've always dreamed of the magic of love, of cozying up with the man of my dreams watching a scary Halloween movie and sharing some popcorn drizzled with caramel. But I don't know how to find that kind of love.

I look up and see a glimpse of sadness in my Aunt Beverly's eyes. "I just want you to find these things that you want," she says, a little quieter and almost speaking to the floor. "Life is short, you know."

My heart slugs and stutters. She's thinking about Henry, her late husband. They were more in love than any other couple I'd seen on this earth, even more than Mr. Seeley and Margie. More than my own parents even. Maybe even more than the people I've read about in all those romance novels.

"You never know when you'll get it or for how long, but it's oh, so worth it," Aunt Bev says with a heavy smile.

Cally walks over and slides her arm around my aunt's shoulders. "Don't worry, Bev. I'll make sure she gets out into the world. It's my personal mission!" Cally pumps her fist in the air.

I sigh, wanting to satiate my aunt's and best friend's hopes for me as well as my own desires. But there is only so much I can do. So much of finding love is out of my control.

"Love is a special kind of magic," I say. "I don't know how it works, really, and I'm sure it'll happen for me someday. It just hasn't come around quite yet. What can I do?"

Cally links her other arm around my elbow and leans her head on my shoulder. "Same here, girlie pop. But I'm still going to do what I can to help you out! Let's talk it out over dinner, yeah?"

I squeeze her hand and nod. "Let's eat and defeat."

CHAPTER 2

Lukas

THE AIR FEELS A BIT MORE SUFFOCATING THAN USUAL IN MY APARTMENT in midtown New York. I look around at the blandness. White walls, white tile, gray couch, no pictures, and nothing on the wall except the TV I watch when I can't sleep at night. I'm not home much anyway, but as strange as it might seem, I don't want to leave.

I toss a handful of plain black dress socks into my black carry-on suitcase. An entire month? How am I supposed to be off work for a whole month? And a reward? Ha. It's more like torture to force me several hours and a few states away from my workplace, the only thing I actually enjoy.

I yank my charger out of the wall and slip my laptop into the side pocket of my suitcase before I zip it up. I glance through the giant window that overlooks New York City. I have a nice view, and I can actually see Fin-vice from here, my workplace for eight years now. It's nice living so close to work. It makes late night commutes less inconvenient.

In the kitchen, I grab a cold water bottle from the fridge and unscrew the cap. Before I can take a sip, my phone is buzzing in my front jacket pocket. I pull it out and see it's just a text from my friend Thomas Martin letting me know the cab is there, and they're waiting for me.

I thumb out a quick reply and slide the phone back into my jacket pocket. With a heavy sigh and even heavier feet, I shuffle to my bed to get my suitcase and figure that I'd better get going downstairs. The closer I get to the ground floor, the more I dread getting into the taxi. But when I finally get there, I set my suitcase in the trunk with a thunk and climb into the backdoor of the taxi where Thomas is waiting, an overly cheerful smile on his face and a sixteen-ounce cup of coffee extended toward me.

"Plain black for the maniac," Thomas teases.

I roll my eyes and take it anyway. "All that extra stuff is just nonsense. I drink coffee for the caffeine, not for the sugary feel-good flavors."

"Oh, Lukas," Thomas sighs, leaning back into the seat and taking a sip from his own cup. It smells faintly of cinnamon.

I don't bother trying to make conversation until we get to the airport, and I get the feeling that I'm getting dangerously close to not being able to bail out of this trip. My stomach is in knots, and as a person who isn't generally anxious, it's unsettling. I just can't fathom leaving work. What else is there to do all day?

"Are you sure this is necessary?" I manage to ask Thomas. We spot the rest of the Fin-vice group by the checked luggage counter. I don't think Thomas is listening to me, so I bump him on the back of the arm. "Hey, man, seriously. Do I really have to do this?"

"I can't say for sure since I'm not your boss or the team leader, but I'm going with yes. You have to do it. It's a team building experience, after all. So, that means the team has to participate. You, my friend, are part of that team," he replies smugly. Then he hesitates and adds, "Plus, I don't wanna be on my own here."

We join the rest of the Fin-vice group, but I don't bother with more than a polite hello. Branden Sharpe, the team leader, gives us the spiel again on why we're doing this. We hit the highest quota in five years this last quarter, and the stats are still looking up. We have a perfectly functioning group, a team of six, and each of us brings something different to the table.

Of course, just as with any team, there is always room for improvement. So, as Branden says, this month-long trip is meant to bring us even closer together, to get to know one another on a more personal level, to better understand one another's strengths and weaknesses. But mostly it's a reward for our performance, so the main goal is to have fun.

I'm not totally convinced, but it seems I'm in it with no easy way out.

While he's talking, all I can do is ruminate. How is taking us away from work supposed to help us perform better? Plus, who takes vacations in September, especially to little dinky Hallmark movie set places with names like Maple Falls, Vermont... for an entire month?

Just then my phone buzzes again. This time it's a client. I'm actually grateful to hear from them, so I can refocus on my work. Everyone else might think this is a time to slack off, but I think it's a good time as any to strengthen bonds with clients and let them know that we'll always be there for them. I type out a quick but thoughtful reply to the Menendez Group accountant supervisor and catch sight of Thomas shaking his head at me.

"Why can't you go more than thirty minutes without answering an email or text?" he asks. His voice is a bit severe, but there's something lingering behind his eyes that tells me he's not just mad or annoyed at me.

I shrug. "I answer because I get the call. That's my job. That's what I get paid for."

Thomas scratches his head beneath his short blond hair. He's always worn a sort of military cut. Guess he never grew out of it after he was discharged.

"Listen to me," he says, almost like he's talking to a scared child. It's a bit unexpected, but I respect him and he's basically my best friend, so I look him in the eye and keep my mouth shut for a few more seconds. "I'm not saying that's a bad quality to have. You're like, really good at all of this stuff." He gestures awkwardly at my phone in my jacket pocket and maybe my suit, too. I tug at it insecurely. "But who even are you outside of work? It's your whole life! I just–can't you just put the texts and emails and reports on the back-burner and just enjoy yourself for the next month?'

His hand is still lingering in front of me like an all-too-nice mosquito looking for an opening. I swat it away. "That's impossible. I don't have the desire to do that." It's true. Work is what keeps me going. "There's nothing to do in Vermont anyway. It's all trees and never-ending roads. How can I enjoy that for an entire month? What does Branden expect me to do? Stare at trees?" I ask, dumbfounded. "That's a waste of time, and you know it. We should be working. I should be working."

Before he can respond, a cadence of rushed stiletto-heeled steps approaches. I already know who it is, and when she places her hand casually on my arm to steady herself, the familiar scent of her perfume hits me like chloroform.

"Wow, I barely made it," Julia Wright says with a laugh. "Glad you guys didn't leave without me." She flips her hair over her shoulder and continues to lean on me. I don't bother looking down at her, but I don't shoo her away either. I'm not in the mood to hear her whine about me being cruel again.

A whole month, huh? Will any of us last that long?

By the time the shuttle gets us from the airport to the little inn in the middle of nowhere, I've been sandwiched between Thomas and Julia for nearly two straight hours. It's strange being close to Thomas, but since we're friends, it's bearable. Julia, on the other hand, keeps pressing her thigh against my leg, and every time we get jostled by a little bump, her hand flies over to my knee.

I've never had a talk with her about boundaries because I have a feeling she's just that kind of person. A little flirty, a little oblivious, the kind that wants constant attention and validation. I think she'd just be the same after the conversation as she is now. So what does it matter?

Instead of feeling suffocated by Julia's incessant touching and Thomas's quiet nonchalance and occasional daggered glances, I focus on my phone. The Menendez Group is considering a big change in financial focus to steer one of their companies in a new direction. I'm curious about it, so how can I take my eyes off my phone while I'm waiting for an explanation of this 'new direction'?

"Curse it!" I mutter. "Why does my service keep dropping like this?"

A feeble little signal bar flickers in and out, teasing me.

"This place better have Wi-Fi or I'm going back right now!" I grunt.

Julia chuckles. "I second that, handsome. The last thing I want is to be stranded out in the boonies with a bunch of hillbillies and no way to call for help."

Thomas rolls his head over. "I don't think it's going to be like that at all." I appreciate that he's a no-nonsense kind of guy. "Branden wouldn't drag us out anywhere sketchy. Just relax and take it all in." He turns back to the window and watches contently.

I decide to see what he's so pleased with and glance out the window. There's a quick flash of a yellowish color, but the vibrating phone in my hand calls my attention back to it. "Sweet," I mutter to myself.

Julia smiles up at me and leans in closer until her chin is essentially resting on my shoulder. I just hope she doesn't leave a makeup stain.

Branden's cheery voice cuts through the silence. "All right, gang. We're about there! We'll have a couple of hours to get settled in and get a tour of our home for the next month. Then the fun stuff starts!"

I grunt and rest my head on the headrest. He was really about to throw us off the deep end, wasn't he? And with that gleeful demeanor. I study his face, his smile. He seems genuine, like he's actually excited to do all of this, and to drag us along behind him. And there's a certain glimmer in his eye that I don't see often. I have yet to decipher whether it's excitement or pure determination. Either way, I can't help but wonder when he'll realize he's over-committed.

A few minutes later, we pull up to the inn, and I practically jump out of the car, desperate to stretch my legs. At least if I get bored, I can just hang out in the exercise room. There's no way I would have agreed to go if they didn't have a place for me to lift and run. I was not okay with returning to New York after losing ten pounds of muscle, and there's no telling how much my stamina will drop if I don't have a treadmill. What a chilling thought.

By the time I grab hold of my suitcase handle, a young woman wearing an oversized, wooly brown pullover and dark brown pants with brown shoes approaches us. She's cute and petite with a wavy brown bob and brown eyes with a smattering of dark freckles across her nose. Even her shoes and hair clip are brown. Is it just me, or is brown perhaps more dull than white and gray?

"Hi, everyone. I'm so glad you made it! How were your travels?" she says as she scans us. Her voice is... not brown. In fact, it's rather... too cheery to be brown.

Branden steps forward immediately and stretches out his hand. "Thank you for having us. We're just ready to get out of the car and get exploring, I think!"

"Oh, you must be Branden Sharpe! It's so good to finally put a face to the name. I'm Ivy Dear, the one you've been emailing with." Her smile is almost bigger than Branden's... almost.

Oh, boy. Two Cheerios in the same vicinity.

Thomas steps forward to offer his hand, which spurs the rest of the team to do the same. I put on my best businessman smile and greet her like a potential client, buttoning my suit's jacket before shaking her hand.

"Wow, you guys are so formal!" Ivy Dear breathes in awe. "We don't usually get this kind of crowd around here."

I hear Julia mutter behind me, "I bet you don't. Has she ever even seen a suit? Or heels?"

After a quick tour of the grounds, which are actually quite extensive, we're chauffeured to our rooms. Mine is on the third floor on the back side of the property. There's a large window in the middle of the room that overlooks the lake and foothills. It is… quiet. The trees all blur together in a mess of yellows and oranges.

"At least I don't have to worry about construction sounds, I guess," I mutter as I check my phone again. The Wi-Fi signal is shaky, but it's there. "As to be expected for being in the middle of nowhere."

I seat myself at the little wooden desk in the corner and get back to the Menendez Group. It seemed like they were ready to attack this new project soon, yet here I am trapped hundreds of miles away for the next month.

And what a long month it's going to be.

CHAPTER 3

Autumn

"Whoa, Auntie. I didn't know you were going to order something cute like this!" I say, pulling out a beautiful green leaf wreath with pops of fuchsia and purple florals, bunches of cream berries, and shoots of grain. Sometimes we get novelty items in, like the Halloween knickknacks that aren't antiques. These wreathes fall into that category as well.

"They're actually made with real preserved flowers," Aunt Bev responds. "That's why they're packed so well."

She studies the side of the wooden crates I've just started unloading, then she opens one and gingerly takes out another wreath.

"I thought you'd like this one," she says, handing it to me. "It's not a hundred percent preserved plants like some of the others, but it reminded me of you."

I take hold of the large wreath and study it with greedy eyes, noticing exactly which part of me my aunt saw in it. The wreath's base resembles that of a bird's nest, a perfect circle with sticks poking out. It is full of fall leaves, but rather than being totally yellow or red, they look like they were plucked off the tree in the middle of changing. They've got hints of golden yellow and orange on the tips, but they're marbled with the green they were trying to gradually eliminate. Some of the golden leaves have dark brown veins running through them, a striking contrast from their bright color. And adorning the mass of leaves are a few little fruits: yellow apples with red speckles, sunrise-yellow and green pears, and even a couple of plump deep pink pomegranates. There's no doubt. It's beautiful.

"Wow, this is so nice," I say, hanging the wreath up gently to display it. "I'm sure it'll sell in no time."

Aunt Bev doesn't say anything. She just looks at me with a mysterious smile playing at the corner of her mouth. "I'll leave you to it so I can man the register for a while."

I nod and get back to work. It's my last full-time day in the store before I start touring. I spend it stocking the new items, like the wreaths we'd just unpacked and some adorable cottage-core embroidered purses, and I make sure everything is tidy. The last shipment of fall items will be here later today, so I also need to make room for the incoming supplies.

I'm in the back of the store about an hour later when the door chime out front rings. And rings. And rings again.

I wonder if it's not some kid running back and forth, or maybe Aunt Bev is trying to take something outside. I step around a shelf of teapots and discover the cause—a group of about six people. But they don't look like ordinary locals. In fact, I haven't ever seen a hoard of black and navy-suited men on the streets of Maple Falls. This place is far too quaint and relaxed. Suits were saved for weddings and holy days at the cathedral. These guys are way overdressed—well, there is one girl who sports a black shin-length pencil skirt and a slim-fitting blazer. She has pinned-up platinum blonde hair and firm, but bright, eyes.

I'm about to go over and help them, but Aunt Bev greets them all, and I hear that they're just looking around and exploring, so I let them be. I'll just keep an eye out if anyone looks like they're interested in something.

Just as I'm about to turn around and go back to the stocking, I hear the door ding again. I glance over my shoulder and see a very handsome man walk through. He's also wearing a suit, but his is deep gray with a dusty blue diamond-pattern tie. He has brown hair that's short on the sides and a bit longer on the top, which is slicked back nicely. I can't help but notice the sharp edge of his jaw, but maybe it's because he's gritting his teeth.

In fact, he looks a little disgruntled, a word I don't often use to describe people around here, and he's staring down at his phone and frowning. He starts to go back outside, but another guy with a blond buzz cut grabs him by the back of his suit jacket and steers him back into the group. The brunette guy concedes but continues to pace around and look at his phone often.

Is he having some kind of family emergency? I wonder.

One of the other men also comes over and says something to him and gets him to smile, but it doesn't meet his eyes. The handsome man puts his phone in his pocket with a look of regret, then looks around the store.

I think I've been watching too long, so I go back to my work. I'm not usually impressed by expensive suits and men who are addicted to their phones. And I've rarely found a brooding, displeased-looking man attractive, but... the way the jacket is so perfectly tailored to his shoulders is distracting. He seems... fit... to say the least. The way the muscles in his jaw tense and release make me want to find out what has him so stressed. And the way his eyebrows draw together, it makes me want to press my finger there and massage slow circles until they go away. I'd seen my mom do this for my father on many occasions. And this guy's lips are pressed together. I wonder why—

Before I know it, I'm looking at him again. Except this time, he's looking at me, too.

I didn't notice when I was scanning him the first time, but his eyes are rich brown, and deep like two wells. I realize we're making fierce eye contact, and my face catches fire.

What am I thinking? I tear my gaze away and start unloading a box of fall harvest- and Halloween-themed children's books to add to the lower tier of the bookshelf.

How could I let my mind wander like that? I know he can't hear what I'm thinking, but I shouldn't have stared at him so long. And was I just thinking about touching this stranger in such an intimate way?! Am I crazy?

I can still feel some heat in my cheeks a couple of minutes later as my mind is still circling around this attention-arresting mystery man. What is he doing here? And who are these people? Why are they dressed so formally? How can a man be built so perfectly for a suit?

I find myself looking back again. He isn't standing in the same spot anymore. As I'm searching for him, I see Aunt Bev with an uncomfortable smile on her face. The impeccably dressed blonde woman is standing near a bin of items we keep near the register in case tourists forget something important, looking at a phone charger, gesturing with her slender hands.

I can hear her voice oozing with confidence and entitlement.

"You really don't have anything better than this useless off-brand charger?" the woman asks brusquely.

Aunt Bev gives her a slight shrug. "I've been using this charger for a while. It charges a phone pretty quickly, so even though it might be 'off-brand,' it's certainly not useless."

The blonde woman grabs the charger from the bin and huffs. "Fine. I guess this will have to do."

It seems like my dear aunt might have been suffering from this lady for a while, so I make my way up to the front and take over at the register. Aunt Bev gives me a tight smile and lets out a pent-up breath. "Thanks, Autumn," she mutters, leaving the register to attend another well-dressed visitor.

"I hope you like this charger. I've been using this brand for about three years, and it still charges my phone pretty fast. If it doesn't work for some reason, you can come back and get a refund," I offer with my best customer service smile.

I don't know what I'm expecting from this woman, but I'm a bit surprised when she just stares at me blankly with her mouth slightly agape and her eyes squinting in disgust.

Instead of saying anything else, I just pick up the charger and scan it.

"There's no chance I'm coming back to this dinky little place," she says as I'm putting it in a little pink paper bag. It doesn't exactly sting that she's called our store dinky, but it certainly doesn't make me like this hard-nosed woman any better. "I'll just buy a better one as soon as I find a real store. I just need to charge my phone now. It's an emergency."

She taps her card against the machine to pay.

"Oh," I say, "If it's an emergency, then you can use our phone–"

But the woman just scoffs and tosses her head back like that's the most ridiculous thing I could have ever said.

"I can't believe I'm stuck here in this annoying simpleton town," she mutters after yanking the bag off the counter.

I watch her strut over to a couple of the men who are waiting by the door.

Oh, one of them is the handsome one from earlier.

The woman goes straight up to him and wraps her hand around his forearm. He looks down and says something to her, but I can't hear it. The blonde looks up at him dreamily with a flirty smile pursed on her lips. Is she literally batting her eyes?

I suppose they're a couple. They're kind of a perfect match, physical appearance-wise. They're both professional-looking, gorgeous— and both have very memorable 'displeased' looks.

I wonder if he's as irritable and inflexible as she is. Oh, well. It's too bad if that's the case.

Just as I'm about to turn around, my sight locks onto an intriguing, rich brown set of eyes. He's looking straight at me. My eyes flutter in response, but I don't look away. I think I see the corner of his mouth tip up, but then his attention is pulled away when he's literally pulled out of the door by the blonde woman.

The door dings closed, and I'm suddenly aware that my heartbeats feel more like palpitations.

CHAPTER 4

AFTER A DREAMLESS NIGHT, I WAKE UP A LITTLE GROGGY. IT'S NOT THAT the mattress is uncomfortable–it's actually pretty nice–but it was just too quiet. I've grown so used to the hustle and honking and constant construction. But here, the silence of the world is on full display. And what am I supposed to do with that?

To wake myself up, I do a couple of sets of pushups and sit-ups then take a shower. Hot showers are for comfort, but I'm looking to be shocked back into reality, so instead, I stand under the cold flow of the rainwater shower head until my body is rigid and covered with goosebumps.

Do I enjoy torturing myself? No, there is nothing pleasing about a cold shower first thing in the morning, but I have to do what I have to do without a hectic office to jolt my mind awake.

Comfort is dangerous.

That's why, when I make it downstairs and it feels like I'm back at my family's home in Nebraska, I'm not sure how to feel. The Hearthlight Inn seems to be all about comfort. It's decently sized, holding ten guest rooms as well as two small meeting rooms, an office that's part library, a separate spacious dining and kitchen area, as well as a sort of game or movie room. And, of course, there's the exercise parlor, as they call it.

Stepping into the dining room, I notice the walls have the same green floral wallpaper that's in one of my favorite restaurants in New York. But here, the wainscoting on the bottom half of the walls has a maple leaf decoration. That's definitely different. The decorations are minimal—gold-framed paintings and floating shelves with vases and books—and it's surprisingly classy. There's a large bay window at the head of the long dining table where I can see a small flock of Canadian geese slinking into the lake.

It's nice enough, but a bit too much like a postcard for me.

"Breakfast is awesome," Thomas says, coming up beside me with a plate in each hand filled with bacon and eggs and waffles and....

"Is that quiche?" I ask, pointing to his plate.

Thomas is wearing a goofy smile and nodding. He shuffles to the table, and that's when I notice that he's just wearing socks on his feet. Actually, he's still in his sweatpants and T-shirt that I'm sure he'd slept in.

He must be comfortable, I think. I flatten my lapel and wiggle my toes self-consciously inside my cognac oxfords. Would everyone else be dressed already? Or would I be the only one put together? I glance around the room, looking for the next sign of life aside from Thomas and Johnathan, who is pulling out a chair next to Thomas.

I'm not very hungry yet, but I know that in the next hour Branden will tell us our itinerary, and this might be my last chance to think for myself for the rest of the day. I decide to check out the breakfast menu, which I find requires ordering at the kitchen window. Apparently, there is wait service for dinner here, but not for breakfast.

When I step up to the kitchen, I have to admit, it smells great. Maybe I am a little hungry.

A man with a bit of gray speckles in his dark hair stands behind the counter. "You look like an omelet kind of guy," he says with an accent that makes me wonder if he also speaks Spanish, lifting a metal spatula and grinning.

I can't help but turn and look behind me, wondering if he's speaking to someone else. But I realize he is indeed speaking to me and he, somehow, is right. I love a good omelet.

I almost crack a full smile back at him. "Yeah, that'd be great. Give me the works, then."

He nods like he knew I was going to say exactly that and goes back to his work. I stand there waiting for the food and feeling a little strange until I spot a coffee station in the corner. A drip brewer sits on the left side of a vintage buffet table with a more than half of a full pot, and beside it a selection of coffee mugs, with images like hot air balloons, #BestDad, Arizona State, and a strange hot pink one with little white bows. It's not exactly classy, but somehow this also reminds me of home. I select the plain black mug and fill it up. Again, I don't bother with cream or sugar.

When I get back to the kitchen window, the chef who'd taken my order introduces himself as Luis and hands me my plate. The moment is quickly over when a familiar clacking of heels on the hardwood draws near. I hear Julia muttering, and I think she's speaking to herself until she rounds the corner, and I see she's on the phone. At least she seems to be primped, primed, and prepared to get on with the day.

I'm not the only one who dressed up.

"I mean, how am I supposed to sleep at night when I can hear every creak and snore and grunt from the room next to me?" she says, complaining.

I plan to walk past her to meet Thomas and Jonathan Clark, another team member, at the dining table, but Julia's face lights up when she sees me, and she sticks out her arm so I can't pass. With her phone still pressed against her ear, she gazes at my face and smiles brightly. She hums a careless response to whomever is on the other end, and I take a step forward. But I'm stopped again when Julia presses her hand to my chest.

"You don't have to tell me twice," she scoffs into the phone. "I'm amazed this phone call has lasted this long. I better go before it drops. I guess I'll see if they have any grease-free options for breakfast... maybe a parfait or something."

I'm getting annoyed, so I use my elbow to gently press her shoulder. "I'm going to sit down," I say, ignoring her phone call. I squeeze my way through, but not before she whines and gives me the down-turned pout she always uses when she wants something from me and I'm brushing her aside.

Thomas and Jonathan have already scarfed down the bulk of their breakfast, but I sit on the other side of them and we make small talk about how we slept and ponder what sort of quests Branden might have for us today. I overhear Julia being rude to the chef. Everyone does.

"Where is our glorious team leader, anyway?" Jonathan asks with a mouthful of blueberry muffin. "Don't we have a meeting soon?"

Before I can answer, Julia saunters over to the table. She plops into the chair next to me, sliding up until her shoulder is pressing into my armpit. "This place is so... boringly simple," she complains. "There's nothing to do. Nothing to eat. And all I see are trees and four-legged creatures."

I press against her to move her over, but I think she mistakes it for permission to get closer because she grins up at me and presses back even harder. I just want to eat my cheesy sausage and mushroom omelet in peace, in my own space.

"You didn't like any of the shops yesterday?" Jonathan asks—again with his mouth full.

Julia is literally taken aback. "You think any of that frumpy frontier land garb would appeal to me? With the ruffles and the floral prints and the cringy little animal pictures?" Her voice is absolutely catty.

It's annoying, but I've learned to numb myself to it. I understand her to an extent. I don't want to be here either, but her incessant complaints and spiteful digs at this town are over the top. Everywhere we went yesterday, Julia went out of her way to make some nasty remark, either passive aggressively or flat out rude.

Plus, there was that one shop with that girl, the place with the color for a name. What was it? I can't remember.

Honestly, the lion's share of my memories from yesterday were of that auburn-haired girl. She was intriguing. Beautiful, with soft features and hypnotizing green eyes. And what caught my attention first was the way she carried herself.

I'd spotted her almost immediately through the window. She was in the back carrying some boxes and unpacking the paper. Her hair is a true auburn, not red and not brown, but a perfect rich mix of the two, worn tied up in a long, wavy ponytail. She walked with nonchalant confidence, never in a hurry. She wasn't distracted. She lived right in the moment. She just... was.

And when she turned around, she was gorgeous.

Her face was perfectly rounded with a cute narrow chin and slightly defined cheekbones. Her nose was a soft slope, and her lips were the epitome of a heart shape–plump in the center with a cupid's bow, looking slightly pursed and ready for....

I clear my throat.

"You good?" Thomas asks.

He's behind me, patting my back. When did he get there, and how long was I just sitting here thinking about that girl?

I clear my throat again for good measure and take a sip of lukewarm coffee.

Julia huffs beside me and crosses her arms. Her lips are a different kind of pursed–tight and trying not-so-hard to keep her annoyance from squeaking out. "Why is it so easy for you to ignore me?" she pouts.

"I'm good," I finally respond, once again, disregarding Julia.

A few minutes later, I'm back in my private bathroom brushing my teeth. My morning had kick-started with thoughts of that beautiful woman, and now I'm fighting for my mind to stay on track. As I stare at myself in the mirror, I wonder whether I could ever carry myself with that kind of effortless tranquility.

I don't understand how anyone could feel like that while living in a small town like this. Back when I was living in Nebraska, in a little town in the middle of nowhere, I felt so stifled, so limited. I was always feeling antsy and ready to move on to something greater, something more. I remember thinking everyone there was just complacent, that they lacked drive. But I wanted to be successful. My parents were supportive enough, but even they were stuck there in the dreary Midwest, especially since Dad is so committed to his work. He still gets up every morning to head to that farm supply company instead of just retiring.

I'm proud to take after him in that way—hardworking and dedicated. But I never wanted to struggle the way he and my mother did. Like we did, despite all Dad's efforts. At least I got out of there. At least I found a place where I could shine and not only support myself, but parents as well. That's success. But why hasn't the weight been lifted from my shoulders yet? Why don't I feel like I can relax now and just stroll through life the way that auburn-haired woman seems to do?

Truthfully, I don't know what would happen if I stop working, or even slow down. I don't know what I would do with my time.

My phone suddenly buzzes on the sink. I expect to see another work email, maybe from the Menendez Group, but it's Julia.

Sit next to me later?

I sigh. Julia is like me in some ways. She works nonstop. But that girl with the auburn hair, she's so different. I wonder what her secret is.

I head back downstairs for the meeting, and as soon as I step off the last stair, Julia grabs my arm. "You didn't answer my message! What do you say, seat buddy?"

"Sorry, Thomas and I are a package deal," I tell her, smacking him on his freshly-suited shoulder with a thud. He turns slowly around to glare at me, but when he thankfully catches the silent pleading in my eyes, he puts on a smile instead.

"Bromances trump all," he says matter-of-factly.

Julia just rolls her smokey shadowed eyes and shifts her weight onto one side. That only means one thing: sass mode activated. I hold my breath, waiting for whatever snarky remark she's going to make, but Branden beats her to the punch.

"What a bright and beautiful morning it is!" he practically sings cheerfully.

Thomas and I exchange a skeptical glance.

"Is this team leader on team vacation or team leader after more than two cups of joe?" I mutter. Either way, it's a lot. Though his job is probably more than I can handle since I didn't get a second cup of joe myself.

Thomas grunts a reply, and the whole crew gathers in the cozy common area with Branden standing in front of the fireplace explaining the day's activities: something about a tour bus and crisp autumn air and getting to know one another's strengths and faults. I don't know what he's really saying, but by the end of his little spiel, half the team is groaning. Julia sighs with exasperation. And while I feel the same way, I can't handle everyone's vexation on top of my own.

"Just take a muffin and try to make the best of it," I tell her, gesturing over to the counter, where a fresh batch of chocolate chip muffins are lined up like a little breakfast army.

She grimaces. "I can't eat carbs like that in the morning."

"I think you'll survive," I respond flatly. "Plus, it's more bearable if you don't resist."

Thomas scoffs. "What is this? Did Lukey have a change of heart overnight?"

Apparently, Jonathan overheard us because he suddenly takes on an encouraging tone. "Yeah, like Lukas said. Let's just try to make the best of it."

I glance around, and a couple of others are nodding their heads in reluctant agreement.

"I think you started a movement," Miles Eskridge, our latest and youngest hire, says with a laugh.

"Now!" Branden attempts to redirect and reignite the group, which is hard to do when we're like a pile of wet, muddy twigs. "Let's hit the road and build an epic team!"

As we're walking out, I spy Chef Luis through the doorway leading into the kitchen sifting flour. In the window where he'd read my omelet-loving soul, I catch sight of a jar with a little laminated sign that says, "Tips." I sneak away from the group for just a moment and shove in a couple of twenty-dollar bills.

CHAPTER 5

Autumn

I step off the tour bus with a little extra spring in my step, my brown platform fisherman sandals crunching into the already fallen leaves. It is the perfect weather to start the tour season. There's a slight bite on the Vermont breeze, and the little whoosh of wind causes a strand of hair to get caught in my lip gloss.

Rookie mistake, I think to myself. But I was just too excited this morning as I got ready for fall's prime time. I wanted to look good, to reflect how I felt about kicking off my first official fall tour of the year. It's my favorite time of year, after all!

I take an extra second to breathe in the fresh air. The wind is carrying a faint ring of the cathedral bell along with the scent of the neighboring cider mill. Ah, Vermont is so beautiful this time of year. How could anyone not fall in love with the lush orange and red leaves filling the forests? Just one drive down the winding roads through that magical atmosphere is sure to rejuvenate anyone's heart. And sharing a fresh, hot cider beside Lake Willoughby, with the fog lifting lazily off the water, certainly stirs up those wistful feelings that the heat of the summer withered out.

Nothing beats the views or the sense of wonder, and I am just so excited to share this with the tourists. Even our local guests often find their eyes careening wildly from the tour bus, desperate to catch every breathtaking glimpse of their beloved hometown. Man, do I have the best job or what?

"You ready to get going?" Gus asks, patting my back gently and knocking me out of my reverie.

Gus Frye has been one of Maple Falls's tour bus drivers for about eight years now, retired from school routes. He has told me that he loved the kids, but he doesn't miss the early mornings and hectic schedules. We're pretty much a package deal at this point. And he's feeling more and more like a grandpa to me every day, always asking about my love life and my health and bringing me goodies that his wife bakes.

I tug at the sleeves of my favorite granola girl sweater and nod back at the old man. "Everything looks good aboard," I say. "Let's go get 'em."

Gus and I make our way back to the tour office, the gravel crunching lightly under our feet. I loop my arm around his. I can't help but notice that he's gotten a tad thinner this year, so I tease him about having to hold him up. He snickers at that, puts his hand atop mine, and gives it a light pat.

"I have a good feeling about this year," he says, a far-off look in his eye. It makes me wonder what he's thinking about specifically, but I don't ask.

Inside, I wave hello to Cathryn Isaacs and Jamal Brown at the front desk. I check the old-fashioned punch clock and can't help but notice two of the other tour guides haven't clocked in yet.

"I can't with those two," I mutter, more than a little annoyed.

Gus catches on immediately and stifles a laugh. "It's been that way since day one with those boys. If they weren't related to the owners, they might not have a job."

I sigh off my frustration at the Grady twins and let Gus slip off to finish up his duties. As a seasoned tour guide, there's not too much I need to do. I already know I'm assigned to the bed-and-breakfast inn. And I could recite the whole trip in my sleep, along with answers to several commonly asked questions. So to hype myself up, I grab a coffee from the break room, squirt on some whipped cream, and sprinkle a dash of nutmeg on top. Just as I'm about to leave, I decide to make a second cup.

A few short minutes later, I reunite with Gus on the bus and hand him the coffee—he's actually the one who taught me how to make it. I was a tea girl before I met him! Cathryn brings over our small group of tourists, and I give them all a hearty welcome. We'll be picking up the rest of our group at the inn. I catch sight of Bethany Howl—third runner-up at the Miss Vermont contest three years ago—and her latest arm candy. He is looking at her adoringly. She nods at me professionally as they climb onto the bus.

Even though I know it by heart, I look down at my itinerary. One spiel about the overarching theme of the tour and one short safety video later, we are off. We zig and zag slowly through the winding roads, and I talk into the microphone connected to the overhead speakers about all the different types of foliage, Vermont's landscape, and some of our city's history. I love seeing the tourists' eyes glow when they catch sight of the autumnal colors. Even Bethany, who has been on these tours a hundred times, seems mesmerized by the amber and fiery red hues the trees have embraced.

When the bus stops at the Hearthlight Inn, I explain the available amenities and the next departure time. I get about a forty-five minute break before it's time to round up the tourists and welcome the rest of our group.

"Autumn!" I hear Ivy call almost as soon as I step off the bus. The little crowd of tourists shuffles down the steps after me and scatter lazily across the property. It's a beautiful, rustic little place, with a large red barn and full garden, and a picturesque lake that reflects the rolling mountains.

"Hi, Ivy," I say, returning her warm smile. She's been a good friend of mine since I started doing the tours.

"Sounds like you're going to have a full bus today!" she says giddily. It's a bit of a reach saying the bus will be full, but having over half the seats filled on the first day of the season had to be a good sign. Her expression drops a bit. "But have you seen the group you're picking up? I wonder what's up with them."

She gestures behind her at the group of about six men who are dressed formally in suits and sunglasses. They seemed familiar to me instantly–the group from the shop. Most of them are muttering at each other, and only two of them really seem to be looking around. I search for the handsome man who was in Aunt Bev's shop yesterday, but I don't see him.

"Company retreat?" I suggest with a shrug.

Ivy nods, gives a little giggle, and pulls on my hand. "I know you can't go far from the bus," she says. "But I want to show you something we've been working on. I think it'll be a real hit once it's ready."

She leads me past the horse stalls and over to a section of the barn that's taped off. She slides one of the giant wooden doors just enough for us to squeeze through.

"What is all this?" I ask, looking around. There are plastic sheets lying on the ground littered with paint splatters and drop cloths, and various vague shapes cover the walls.

"Well, one thing everyone always wants is an experience, right? And they want mementos, a moment they can capture and take with them. So, this will be a photo room! It's gonna cost a pretty penny to set up, but I'm hoping that it'll really take off and be an extra bit of income. Guests will be able to choose one of two rooms where they can take pictures by themselves. It's a little bit like a photo booth but with more room and props! I've been seeing a lot of this kind of thing on social media, and my parents thought it might be worth a try."

I smile. "That sounds cool. I have to be honest. It's hard to imagine with all the plastic on the ground, but it sounds fun! I don't think we have anything like that around here."

Ivy and I chat some more about the inn and the efforts they're making to become a must-see spot in Vermont. Before long, the forty-five minutes have passed. It's time to board the bus again.

Ivy walks me back to the big brown bus before she jets back off to her favorite place, the barn.

I hope her idea is successful. It certainly sounds like something people will love.

A few minutes later, I glance down at my watch. We're nearly five minutes over time, and only two-thirds of the tour group have boarded. I glance through the open bus doors at Gus, who shrugs his shoulders and goes back to conversation with a middle-aged couple sitting behind his driver's seat.

When the tourists finally come out at eight minutes past the hour, I see that it's the group of businessmen. One of them looks quite enthusiastic, and he's talking over his shoulder to someone behind him. He taps a pen on the clipboard he's holding and passes it behind him.

"This place is just the start!" the enthusiastic man says as he approaches me. His well-dressed buddies file onto the bus slow as molasses. "Hi there," he says, jutting a hand out to me. "I'm Branden Sharpe."

Shake his hand and admire the clothes he's wearing, even though they're also a tad fancy for our planned trip in the country. So this is what a pin-striped suit looks like… and his shoes look like real Italian leather. Very fancy.

"It's nice to meet you," I say politely. "I'm Autumn Ackerman. I think I saw you all in my aunt's antique store yesterday. It's called Blue Kiss."

"Yes!" Branden cheers like I just sparked a core memory long forgotten. "Wow, it really is a small town if you've already seen us twice!" He continues to shake my hand enthusiastically.

I contain my smirk, thinking I didn't expect any one of these people to be so chipper and completely into this tour, especially after how the blonde woman acted in our store.

Just then, the clipboard Branden was holding appears between us. And attached to the arm holding it out… a familiar stranger. The man is even more handsome today, however that's possible. I feel the heat rise in my cheeks and wonder whether I should say anything to him.

I gulp, trying not to lose my professional cool. "I hope you enjoy the tour," I say, glancing up to meet the man's steady, heavy gaze. He's not smiling, but there's a hint of something deep in his cavernous brown eyes that makes it hard to look away. He lets the clipboard fall back into his coworker's hands and gives me the slightest hint of a smirk before he passes and steps up into the bus.

From within, I hear a woman's voice. "Lukas! What on earth took you so long? I've been sitting here by myself for hours because my heels were hurting my feet."

Branden excuses himself, and we both enter the bus. I can see now that Lukas is talking with none other than the platinum blonde businesswoman. Or rather, he was being talked to by her.

"The bus hasn't even been here for an hour," Lukas replies, sliding into the seat on the other side of the aisle from her. "That's a bit of an exaggeration, don't you think?"

Did they have an argument? I wonder.

"And I can smell the stink of those beasts from here!" she continues. "Can't we get a move on now?"

"Why did you even come if you're just going to complain?" Lukas asks. Somehow his voice is neither chiding nor annoying. It's amazing that he can have such patience for a woman like that. And that just makes me even more curious about him.

Suddenly, Lukas's eyes flick to me. I feel the heat in my cheeks spring back to life immediately.

I clear my throat and ensure we've got all our tourists back on the bus. Now that I'm aware of this striking man, I'm finding it difficult to pass my gaze to each passenger evenly. I just hope nobody notices that my voice keeps getting stuck in my throat or that my skin is growing more tomato-like every moment I'm standing in this new man's presence.

Get a hold of yourself, woman! The stern version of me says in the back of my mind. *You're going to embarrass yourself. Have you never seen a hot guy before or something? He's just a guy!*

I suck in a breath and push back my overactive mind. Stern Me is right, though. This guy is just a guy! A tall, broad-shouldered, jaw like a razor and eyes like a deep cavern-ed guy.

With a girlfriend, Stern Me juts back in.

I force my eyes on a family of three sitting at the back of the bus who had departed with us from the bus stop. "The next stop is a classic one, the local Smithson Apple Orchard!" I announce. "Who here enjoys apple pie?" The kid in the back looks up at his mom, and I decide to make another suggestion. "How about some toasty warm cider?"

CHAPTER 6

MAYBE IT'S THE WAY AUTUMN, THE TOUR GUIDE, IS EXPLAINING everything in such detail and care and genuine passion that I find myself actually kind of enjoying the tour. I'm not sure if Autumn is her real name or not, but it sure is fitting. Visually, she seems like she could be the embodiment of autumn.

Now on the bus, when she's speaking to us, I hang on to every word she says, and I don't have to look away. It's natural to look at someone when they're talking to you, especially when they're feeding you information like a warm potato soup. So I do. I can study her a little more now that she's closer to me than she was in the store yesterday.

Today, her hair is down, auburn waves cascading down her back to the bottom of her shoulder blades. Her hair swings softly as she gestures out the window and explains how the leaves change color. It's like a third-grade level explanation, but it's fascinating to listen to in her exquisite voice. Carotenoids and anthocyanin and energy conservation–the way she describes it all, every word intrigues me.

As does her smile. This is the first time I'm seeing it, and I can't rip my eyes away. It's probably the most beautiful thing I've seen since... well, maybe ever. She doesn't have dimples, but when her lips stretch back, faint smile lines appear on both sides symmetrically. And her eyes, I see now, are green, the same color as healthy leaves before they start to turn.

"Dude," I hear Thomas say almost directly into my ear.

I startle a little, more from the sudden closeness and the percussive feeling than from the sound. "What the heck?" I yelp a bit too loudly. I glance back up to the front of the bus to see if Autumn caught that reaction. If she did, she's not showing any sign of it.

"I know this is like, enlightening information we're getting," Thomas says dryly. "But don't you think ogling the tour guide is a bit...."

He stops his sentence, and his semi-judgmental glare slowly slips into amusement. "You got a little crush on our tour guide, don't you?" he says smugly.

I roll my eyes. "Crushes are for middle schoolers."

"Julia is gonna be so upsetti-spaghetti," he whispers.

"Why are you bringing up Julia?" I ask, growing a little peeved.

Thomas sighs and leans back in his seat, but keeps his voice low. "Honestly, Lukas. Can't you tell she's totally into you? Anyone can see it."

I just shrug. Julia is the least of my worries. "She's just like that because I helped her out one time a couple years ago. It's just her weird way of showing gratitude or something. Like she trusts me or whatever."

Only looking more intrigued, Thomas is about to say something prying, I'm sure, but one of our fellow teammates asks a question about the forest. Autumn takes the questions graciously and doesn't hesitate to give an engaging answer. She's so animated when she talks about this little town and these tree-covered mountains. All I can say is that she really must love this place and what she's doing, or she's a really good actor. I don't think it's the latter.

I imagine this sort of job doesn't pay well. Plus, she seems to work at that shop. The Blue… ugh, I just can't remember what it was. Either way, giving tours and working in a little shop like that surely wouldn't bring in much of an income. It's rare for people to willingly work two jobs unless they just really need the money or truly love what they're doing.

It makes me a little more curious about her. She seems like such a good sport.

"Oh! This bridge we're about to cross over is a famous landmark here in Maple Falls," Autumn starts up excitedly. She leans her hand on the seat in front of her. I can't help wishing I'd been sitting there to get a closer look at her, and to get another whiff of her perfume. I also have to admit that I am a bit annoyed that the people who are in that seat aren't even looking at her when she's talking so fervently. "This bridge, which has been painted cerulean blue for over one hundred years, is known locally as The Kissing Bridge."

All I can do is stare, and want to know more. So, I sit forward in my seat slightly, resting my forearms on my knees. The bus slows, along with my heartbeat, as I watch her expand on the concept.

"You're probably wondering if it got its name for being a romantic spot, and while that has come to be true over the last few decades," she adds. "It actually got its name because the bridge sits so close to the water that anyone trying to pass under in little fishing boats and canoes would have to lean forward to avoid hitting their heads," Autumn explains. "During the rainy season, boats aren't allowed because the water is too high, but this little creek is generally safe, and so couples might come here for a stroll or to picnic near the water."

For maybe the first time since the tour started, I look out the window. We're passing over a wide bridge with beams painted a warm summery blue. It contrasts strikingly with the yellow trees that surround it and lean over the water's edge. I see that the bridge is wide enough for two car lanes, and there is also a sidewalk-sized path on each side for foot traffic.

"Wow," I mutter.

"Isn't it great?" Autumn gleams. For a half a moment, I think she's responding to me. "This bridge has a soft place in my heart, as I'm sure it does for many other townsfolk here in Maple Falls."

That catches my attention. A soft place? In her heart? Perhaps she already has a boyfriend. Of course, I wouldn't be surprised at all by that. She seems… captivating, in more ways than one.

At the back of the bus, a young boy raises a hand and asks, "Why is this bridge special to you?"

My throat tightens, certain that her response will be that the love of her life first kissed her here in this spot.

"My aunt and uncle got engaged on this bridge," she answers. Her smile droops a little, like there's some invisible weight behind it. "They had the most beautiful relationship I've ever witnessed. So my aunt always says it's good luck if a proposal happens on a blue bridge."

Had. She said it in past tense.

Before I can linger on what sort of sadness lurks behind this story, Autumn perks up again as we're getting to the other side of the creek. "This bridge is also a marker for our next stop! That's right, guys. We're approaching the Smithson Apple Orchard! As I mentioned, this orchard has been owned by the Smithson family for six generations! And it's an iconic spot to spend many fall days."

There she is again, glowing as though everything about this job infuses life into her.

Meanwhile, I can't think of anything that excites me that much. Not about New York. And not even about work. I've always focused on work because that's what I like to do, so I don't know much about the city I've called home for ten years. Does it make me glow like her? Does it make me feel alive? I've never really thought about that before.

At the orchard, I realize just how poorly dressed I am for the occasion. I suppose we fit the role of a bunch of city slickers in small town USA wearing our suits and dress shoes. We only get a couple of strange looks from the other tourists, but Autumn treats us all the same. Not that I've even talked to her yet… In fact, I'm not sure she's made eye contact with me since the bus took off. That stings a little, but I suppose I'm not much her type considering the different worlds we come from.

For the next hour, our assignment is to wander around the orchard and pick our own baskets of fruit. It's not just apples here. There are pear trees as well as beds of marigolds and lavender strung between the rows of trees. It's fragrant and fresh and… am I starting to like the feel of sunshine on my hair? Ha. That is highly unlikely.

I'm grateful to Thomas for sitting next to me on the bus so I didn't have to sit next to Julia. She's a bubble encroacher if there ever was one, and it really seems like this trip has just magnified that trait. As soon as we were off the bus, most of the Fin-vice group split up to explore on their own. I feel bad for using Thomas as my scapegoat, so I let him go, too. Now all I have to do is casually steer clear of high-heel clad women, and I'll be fine.

I slip out my phone and glance at it. I hadn't checked it since we left the inn, which is uncharacteristic, to say the least. There are no new emails from the Menendez Group, probably because I don't have service here. I suck in a long breath and let it out for even longer. Then, I take a look around.

It is quite beautiful here. I sort of like the way the sun shines through the trees, casting down little beams of light through the leaves. The distant sound of small talk and the faint buzzing of a few insects remind me of my home in Nebraska. But that seems like so long ago. The memory is more bogged down and coated in dust than this scene before me.

Down the row of trees I'm walking past, I see Miles, Jonathan, and my buddy Thomas chatting and laughing. They've all shed their jackets, and Miles has his jacket draped over his shoulder. They really seem to be enjoying their time here. I might envy them a little for that.

"What's going on here?" I ask as I approach. I point and stifle a laugh when I spot the little woven basket in Thomas's hands. It looks so out of place.

"You gotta try this," Jonathan says, tossing a shiny red apple at me. "It's the best thing you'll ever taste. Guaranteed."

I turn the apple over in my hands. It's a bit smaller than most I'd picked up at the produce stand by my apartment in New York, but it's also heavier. I glance to my left. "Is that allowed?"

"Weren't you listening?" Miles says. "That's the whole point of being here. We look at apples. We pick apples. We eat apples. We buy apple-flavored baked goods."

I roll my eyes at him.

"It's fine. Eat all you want," a light voice says from behind me. It's a new kind of familiar, and I swivel around. Autumn is carrying a basket of her own, loaded up with apples and pears alike. She's smiling at us, at me. "Don't be shy about it."

The boys chuckle behind me. I really want to say something to her, but I'm too distracted with the way her hair shimmers whenever a beam of sunshine hits it, and wondering how long she'd been walking behind me.

Suddenly, she meets my eyes. It's only for a quick second before she looks down and continues past us. I catch sight of pink on her cheeks. She's blushing. It isn't quite warm enough for that blush on her cheeks to be from exertion.

"In that case–" Thomas says joyfully as he grabs hold of my shoulders and gives them a firm shake. "Let's see who can pick the most!"

"Not just the most," I counter. "The best."

I shrug off my jacket and roll up my sleeves.

Autumn peeks over her shoulder, and I catch her covering a laugh. It lights a little fire in me.

If I'm going to pick apples, I'm going to find the best ones. The crispiest, juiciest, reddest ones, to match the color of that fiery auburn hair.

CHAPTER 7

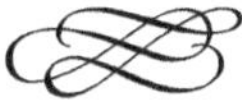

IT'S EARLY IN THE MORNING, SO EARLY I CAN STILL SPOT A FEW STARS overhead. The waning moon has taken on a muted butter yellow color but still provides me with enough light to take Tess, my dachshund, down the street. Again. For the fourth time, actually. The moonlight is gleaming faintly off her black back, and her nails scratch against the sidewalk as she paces back and forth from grass to street to grass on the other side of the street.

We have to be going on twenty minutes, I'm thinking. The warmth of my bed is beckoning me, and I just want three more hours of sleep. But I don't control Tess's bladder any more than I can control an earthquake. I'm glad she doesn't do this more often at four in the morning. But even if she did, she's so cute and such a snuggle bug, I don't really mind, even if I need to lose a bit of sleep.

A couple of minutes later, Tess finally gets down to business. And while we're on the way back, probably a good block from home, my thoughts wander. A haunting set of eyes pops into my head, followed by the rest of the most handsome man I've ever seen.

Lukas. I haven't decided yet whether his name suits him, but I'm happy to know who he is now. Thanks to my keen ears and Branden, the team leader, I have a name to put to the face. I didn't see him and that blonde business-level bombshell talk much at all during the tour, so I think I might have been mistaken about them being together.

If that is the case, I can consider talking to him some more. And it may be my imagination–or wishful thinking–but I feel like he might have wanted to talk to me, too.

As much as I was trying to avoid it, I kept sensing his eyes on me the whole time we were on the bus. I couldn't swallow my pride and look at him like any of the other passengers. And then I couldn't muster up the courage to say anything to him when I was following behind him in the orchard like a quizzical duckling. It was only the moment he met with his friends that I found my voice, but even then, I couldn't do more than meet his gaze for a few lousy seconds.

Actually, those seconds weren't lousy at all. They were a little magical, maybe. Perhaps I've been reading too many romance novels again, but I sort of felt a spark, or maybe a zing, when we locked eyes. And when he parted his lips as if to say something to me, I just smiled and walked away.

Who does that?! I scream internally, regretfully.

Tess leads me around the back of Blue Kiss, past the makeshift haystacks and the little scarecrow guarding the mums and into the backside of the shop. She runs ahead of me as we head up the stairs and into my studio apartment. Even though I'm pretty much the only one up here, I'd splurged and got that beautiful autumn wreath my aunt said made her think of me for my door. I run my fingers gently over it before stepping inside and letting Tess off the leash. She dashes off into the dimly lit apartment, her dog tag jingling along the way.

As I crawl into bed and slip my feet under the covers, which have already grown a bit cool again, I force Lukas out of my mind. Now isn't the time to get caught up on a sharply dressed, handsome man with electrifying eye contact. Plus, I still remember my first impression of him. He was tense and severe looking, not exactly the warm and friendly type. But then again, even if it was in passing just a couple of times, there was that soft, boyish grin when he was talking with his co-workers. Maybe I'd just caught him on a bad day.

The truth is, I won't know either way. And who knows if I'll ever see him again. He's here for vacation, not to cozy up with an enthusiastic fall tour guide.

That sort of thing doesn't usually last long anyway.

I shimmy myself deeper under the covers and squeeze my eyes shut. I need to focus on other things. Like today because it's Cally's birthday. I got her the perfect present, and I can't wait to give it to her. Plus, this little party is a good excuse to wear one of the cute sweaters I recently bought.

I pop an eye open to look at the digital clock on my bedside table, which reads 4:24 A.M. Just a few more hours and I can start Cally's birthday off right! I have a whole thing planned for her. A girl only turns twenty-five once, after all.

And as I slowly drift off to sleep, my mind keeps dodging images of deep brown eyes and a perfect set of stern lips, and ponderings about whether I might run into the owner of those near the inn, where I happened to know he is staying... and where Cally's birthday celebration happens to be.

Cally and I have plans for a late breakfast at Rudy's. On her days off, Cally never wakes up before 10:00. Meanwhile, last night I tossed and turned and finally crawled out of bed at 6:09 A.M. With the misguided idea of getting my body moving, I decide to take a run.

I don't make it more than twelve blocks before I'm winded, but Tess somehow has energy to spare, so we walk through the park in the middle of town and back. When I get home, I take a long shower, taking care to deep condition my hair so I can make myself look nice for the occasion.

For Cally's birthday, that is, not for that other person I might run into....

Mr. and Mrs. Stein planned the party in the event near the Hearthlight Inn. It's all owned by Ivy's family, with a row of sycamore trees and a cute white fence that separates the main bed-and-breakfast with the party venue. Apparently, Cally's parents want to give their daughter somewhere different to celebrate other than their restaurant, Maple Falls Café, where they have it almost every year. Some friends of theirs are also caterers, so they've planned the whole thing so Cally and her parents can relax and enjoy the night. It's time for Cally to get waited on for a change.

It might seem odd to some people, a twenty-five-year-old letting her parents plan her birthday party, but that's just the kind of relationship they have with their daughter. They know her heart and mind inside and out. Plus, they have a lot of connections to make the logistics work. I always offer to help, but they have it covered every year.

When we arrive, it almost seems like the party was spawned from my brain rather than Cally's parents. Then again, we've all always bonded over the beauty of fall. Her party is like a mini fall festival. Music plays over a couple of outdoor speakers hidden behind some small square bales of hay. There is a large bonfire getting started out in the middle of the lawn behind the event hall, and it's already surrounded by camping chairs and logs to sit on. There are a few knit blankets and quilts laid out on the ground. Close by is a table labeled 'The S'more the Merrier.' A few yard games are already at play: cornhole, horseshoes, jumbo Jenga, and—oh, my goodness–pumpkin carving?! I am definitely going to be getting into that ASAP.

Inside the venue, there's also a long wooden table filled with chili, cornbread, pie, and green bean casserole, along with too many other comfort foods to list. Next to the food table is a drink stand, complete with hot chocolate, apple cider, punch, and some alcoholic beverages for the adults.

My favorite part, though, is the strings of lights illuminating the evening. The sun has yet to set, but already the lights cast a dreamy glow from the event building with its giant sliding glass door opened up, all the way out to the bonfire.

"Your parents really went all out this year!" I say to Cally, clasping her arm.

She squeezes my hand excitedly, a large toothy smile plastered on her face. "This is the best one yet. I can tell!"

While Cally is making her rounds saying hello to her friends and family, Ivy finds me and hands me a toasty cup of cider. Some people probably feel it's still too warm for hot drinks since the temperature has yet to get below 65 most days, but I'm all in.

"You look super hot, by the way," Ivy says candidly, scanning me up and down. "How long have you been hiding those nicely toned arms and legs?"

Yeah, maybe this cute little off the shoulder sweater and denim mini skirt mix have something to do with it. "Oh, well, Cally helped me get ready. This is really mostly her handiwork," I reply.

Ivy gives me a simple smile and a soft shake of her head, dismissing my dismissal of her compliment. "Let's get in there," she says, looping her pinky around my pinky and pulling me along behind her, the way she often does.

We snatch Cally away from a group of well-wishers and pull her toward the refreshments. After swinging by the drink table, where Cally grabs a warm cider, we find our way to the pumpkin carving area. Maybe it seems childish to some, but this is our element. Cally and I have been friends for a long time, but we've been pumpkin carving rivals for even longer. It all started at the Autumn Leaves Celebration nearly twenty years ago. I beat her triangle-nosed jack-o'-lantern in the kiddy division with a classic buck-toothed, moon-eyed jack-o'-lantern. And we'd been competitive ever since, at least as far as pumpkin carving goes. One of us usually won the contest, and the designs are getting more complex every year.

But for today, we save the antics and just have fun. The real challenge will come in the next month when the Autumn Leaves Celebration arrives. So instead of our pumpkin duel, we hang out with some of Cally's younger cousins. Meena, age ten, Jack, age eight, and little

Jihwan, who has only just turned six. Jihwan plops himself in my lap, and I help him carve out the top of the pumpkin. He comes out with double fists of pumpkin guts and loves every second of it. Thanks to an ingenious invention called an apron, I'm feeling relatively safe from the mess.

"Are you going to dress up for the festival this year?" Cally asks.

Jihwan is too focused to answer, but Meena nods enthusiastically. "I'm going as Ha-nana, one of the characters from a video game I like!"

"Let me guess," Ivy deadpans. "She's a strawberry."

Meena rolls her eyes and smacks her lips. I wonder if she learned that from Cally or from her mother. Either way, it's hilarious. "Obviously, a banana. It's basically in the name."

Ivy and I share a knowing look.

"What about you, Jack?" I ask.

He's a quiet kid, taking his time to form a perfect circle on the pumpkin. "Train conductor," he replies.

"Haven't seen that one before!" I realize. "That'll be cool."

I get a soft smile out of him, but he never looks away from his pumpkin.

"What about you guys?" Meena asks.

"Miss Congeniality," Ivy says matter-of-factly.

I laugh. It's kind of perfect for her in a strange way. I love it. Cally says she'll be a monarch butterfly with a twist, and I wonder what that means, I realize it's my turn to answer.

"I haven't quite figured that out yet," I explain.

Thankfully, I spot Cara, Cally's mom, looking a little frantic. "Looks like your mom needs some help," I say. I transplant Jihwan into Ivy's lap and go over to her.

"What's the matter?" I ask when I've made my way to Mrs. Stein.

"Oh, Autumn, honey, could you help me out, please?" she asks, tapping my elbow lightly. "I was just on my way to refill the punch, but Mr. Dominguez told me that his son burned his hand on the fire-stones. Could you please get the punch refilled while I tend to Robert?"

"Sure thing," I reply.

She explains that the punch canisters are back in the Inn's kitchen, which is where the caterers have been preparing all the food. I pass through the side door of the event building to cut across the wooded landscape. By now, the sun has set halfway, and on this side of the building under the sycamore trees, there's not a lot of light. And before I see any signs of life, I hear a nearby crunch in the grass. It doesn't sound like a little one, either.

A fact suddenly pops into my head: Vermont has the densest population of black bears in the country.

Wow, good timing with that reminder, brain.

I've only seen two bears in my whole life living here, and it's not likely that a bear would come so close to a loud gathering, though it certainly isn't impossible.

I say a silent prayer and do exactly what you're not supposed to do: run.

I don't get far before I crash into something solid. I'm about to scream, but since when do bears say, "Oof?"

A pair of strong hands takes hold of my shoulders. Warm, strong hands.

"You okay?" the man says. Yeah. It's a man. Not a bear. I feel the tension filter out of my body until I look up at the man's face.

It's the same handsome face that has been testing my ability to fall asleep at night.

CHAPTER 8

I'm surprised to see Autumn there at the inn, and it seems she's surprised to see me, too. Seconds before I was about to call out to the shadowy figure walking toward me, she darted straight at me. The last thing I wanted was to scare her, but now she's looking up at me with a mix of shock and relief, her eyes fluttering quickly and her breath stuck in her throat.

"You okay?" I ask, my hands on her shoulders to steady her.

I quickly realize I'm touching her, and that was probably more than she bargained for from a stranger in the dark woods, so I remove them quickly. They hover somewhere between us, not quite sure where to land.

"Oh, my gosh," she finally breathes. "I thought you were a bear."

I can't help but smirk. "Not the worst thing I've been called, so I'll take it."

Although it's a bit dark out, I can tell by the way she's lightly bowing her head that she's a little embarrassed.

"It's reasonable to be afraid, I think, considering a tour guide recently told me that Vermont has like the biggest, densest bear population in the United States," I add, putting my hands in my slacks pockets.

I hear a little puff of air, a charming release of tension. "What're you doing out here?" she asks.

I shrug. "Just came out for some air and heard the commotion in that building. Thought I'd check it out." I don't need to tell her I was also on the hunt for better cell service. "What's going on over there, anyway? Sounds like fun."

Autumn turns her face to glance behind her, and the dim light slides over the curves of her face. Though I still can't see her well, it's enough to make me stop as my train of thought crashes into a deep canyon.

"It's my friend's birthday party," she explains. "They went all out this year. It's like fall festival practice."

"Interesting," I respond, listening more to the sound of her voice than the words themselves. It reverberates gently, light and easy, as if she narrates nightly Bible stories or meditation podcasts.

"I was just heading over to the Hearthlight Inn to get some more punch for the drink table." She pauses for a second and faces me again. "Then I ran into you."

My mind snaps back into the moment. "I'm so sorry about that. I'm sure you didn't expect to run into a stranger out here."

I hear that breathy release again. "This is the third time we've met. You're closer to acquaintance than stranger."

It seems like my heart is thumping in slow motion. "Is that right?" I ask, all too pleased with her answer.

"Well." I clear my throat. "If I help you out with this punch situation, do you think I can graduate to an official acquaintance? Or maybe even... a friend?"

"Okay," she says simply. "But if we really do meet a bear out here, your reaction will grossly determine the status of our relationship."

Oh, I would tackle that bear and put it in a headlock for you, I don't dare say out loud.

"Though–" Autumn draws out the word. "I think both your fight and flight might be hampered by your… wardrobe."

Is she teasing me? Because if so, I love it.

"You'd be surprised," I say. "I can lift my arms to… here." I slowly raise my arms until they're about a thirty-degree angle.

This elicits an adorable chuckle. "I'm saved," she says through her laugh.

I can't help but smile along with her. I put my arms down, and the two of us walk toward the inn.

"My name is Lukas, by the way," I say. "Your name is memorable, Autumn."

She smiles at me again and nods. "Fits the vibe, doesn't it?"

Our feet swish through the grass and crunch an occasional twig. In the natural space between the party barn and the inn, the air is still and quiet except for the sounds of our slow footsteps and our light-hearted small talk.

"I've only seen a bear two times in all my life," Autumn confesses. "And both times I was looking from the safe side of the window. So, I truly don't have a clue how I'd react."

"Well, I've never seen a bear outside of a zoo, so I'm probably worse off than you," I joke. "Plus, there's the whole suit thing."

"You were wearing a suit the last two times I saw you as well," she notes. "Is it glued to your skin or something?"

Honestly, it feels that way sometimes. When was the last time I wore anything other than suits or running shorts? "You see… I have no explanation at all, other than this is what I wear to work, and I work every day of the week."

She flicks a glance over my body, which makes my skin turn rigid. "Do you sleep in it, too, then?"

It's my turn to laugh. "Are you like this with all of your acquaintances?"

Autumn doesn't respond, but she gives me a coy lift of her eyebrows instead. "So, work…. What is it? Are you a CEO or something?"

"Nah," I say coolly. "I'm just a financial advisor for a big corporation called Fin-vice."

"Oh, punny," she mutters softly.

My mouth twitches up. I had thought the same thing.

"And you guys are from New York?"

I just nod. For some reason, I always struggle to tell people I'm from New York. I've lived there for ten years with no eye for anywhere else, but I don't know much about the place. I rarely visit my parents in Nebraska, so I don't really feel like I can say I'm from there, either.

"What's the big city like?" she asks. "I've traveled a bit with my parents, but never to New York."

Again, I don't really know what to say. "It's... noisy? There are a lot of people and pigeons. Cars everywhere. Crazy subway system."

Suddenly, Autumn stops. I start to look around, thinking maybe all this talk about bears has finally attracted one. I stop, too, and roll my shoulders slightly.

"Are you sure you're from New York?" she says. The light poles from the inn aren't far from us now, so I can see that she's squinting at me in a comically suspicious way. "It seems like you're just giving me all the New York stereotypes that I've seen in the movies and in books."

"True, but it's a city of stereotypes," I reply.

"Okay, then," she says, slowly resuming our walk. Really, we're strolling, taking our time. And I don't even wonder if the party is puttering out because of the lack of punch. "Rapid fire. What's your favorite place in New York?"

I can't answer right away. Do I have one?

"Rapid fire! That means quickly, Mister Financial Advisor."

I suck in a breath. "Maybe... the park I take runs in?"

"Favorite restaurant."

Another pause.

"You're really not good at this," Autumn jests.

I don't mind that she's teasing me. I like it. It makes me feel like we're friends already.

"There's good carryout Japanese food next to Fin-vice," I offer.

As we approach the back entrance of the inn, Autumn pauses once again and turns to face me. In the full glow of the porch light, and with the moon helping out overhead, I see she's got a bit of color in her cheeks. Is she cold? Feeling shy?

I study her, seeing her fully now. She's wearing her hair half up with all of it slid behind her back. If she's wearing makeup, I can't really tell aside from the slightly more pink tint of her lips and the fullness of her eyelashes. Her sweater is black and slouchy, hanging off one shoulder and pulling my gaze to her collarbone. I take just a second to notice her skirt, and more specifically, her legs, which are hard to miss.

I find her eyes again, and her face is slightly more flushed now. "You should really relax," she says. "You're in Maple Falls now, not New York City."

I'm about to answer her, or maybe tell her I'm sorry for letting my eyes linger and wander, when a very untimely beep of my phone goes off. Instinctively, I reach for it, but I can feel Autumn watching me with curiosity rather than scorn or suspicion.

It beeps again. It could be the Menendez Group. We had just started talking about a seven-step business plan to get their new company up and running....

Great time to get good cell service all of a sudden, I think.

"Do you need to get that?" Autumn asks. "I'll just go in and—"

"No!" I say quickly, taking a step up toward the door. "It can wait. Let me help you."

For once, maybe I believe what I'm saying. While I'm not sure what is happening between us just yet, I want to learn more about Autumn and Maple Falls. I want to give her my undivided attention, even if it might be unwanted. It doesn't seem that way—she's had a couple of chances to tell me I was bothering her, and she hasn't.

"Let's go then," she says, leading the way inside.

Inside, we find a mess of caterers, and Autumn pulls one aside to ask about the punch situation. After a short exchange of words and a trip to the giant walk-in fridge, Autumn and I walk out with three huge sealed containers of red punch.

When Autumn tries to take two, I hold out my hand. "It's my duty as a gentleman to carry more than the lady."

I get a sheepish smile out of her when she relinquishes two containers to me.

On the way back, she tells me about Maple Falls, how she has lived here her whole life and can't imagine wanting to be anywhere else. How she graduated from high school as Most Likely to Win the Lottery but Lose the Ticket, and that she was also the Salutatorian. She had attended the local college the next town over, driving back and forth every day. And she has recently earned a dual degree in liberal arts degree and earth science. She told me the basics about her dachshund Tess, and her nationwide-traveling parents.

The party is still in full swing when we get to the event hall, but I can hardly pay attention to it. After we fill the metal canisters with all three containers of punch, Autumn reaches out and touches my wrist light as a leaf. "Do you want to stay?" she asks.

There goes that slow-motion thumping again....

I certainly feel tempted, especially after hearing her talk so much about herself. I really like the way she seems in awe of everything. I feel I can learn a thing or two from her.

"I'd hate to intrude. After all, I'm barely an acquaintance of yours," I say.

Autumn shrugs and lilts her head slightly to one side. "I don't know. I think we could be friends."

I give her a smile I can't hold back. "Still, I'd hate to intrude on the birthday party. But I'd love to talk more with you," I say. "Perhaps over dinner?"

Autumn sucks in her lips to hold back a smile. "Are you asking me on a date? That would probably go beyond 'friends.'"

"Yes," I say matter-of-factly. "A date."

She grows quiet and takes her hand slowly away to tuck her hair behind her ear. I catch a glimmer from her earring that shines on her cheek. "And Miss Platinum Blonde on Stilettos won't mind?"

I furrow my brow. There's only one person she could be talking about. "Julia? Why would she matter?"

Autumn ducks her head adorably. "I just thought you guys might be... involved."

I can't help but laugh. "No. Julia's nothing but a colleague, and a challenging one at that. So, what's your answer?"

She gives me a good-natured grin. "Fine, then. It's a yes."

I keep my inward celebration to myself.

"But we're going to have to take you by the department store first," she says, smoothing her hand over my lapel. "Step one in learning to relax: comfy clothes."

"I'm all in."

CHAPTER 9

Autumn

Is this even real? I'm about to go on a date... with a really, really handsome man from New York, a businessman who I've only ever seen in a suit, even though he's supposedly on a team vacation. I can't say that I ever expected this moment to take place in my life.

But here I am wearing my second favorite sweater because I can't possibly have Lukas see me in the one I wore for Cally's birthday yet again. This time I'm going for casual-cutie-on-the-sly, as Cally would call it. The outfit of choice is an earthy sage green sweater with a wide boat neck, and medium wash jeans that hug my waist and hips and loosen up at the leg. To dress it up, I've opted for a pair of vintage square-toed white boots to give me a little edge.

As I swipe on my mascara and catch sight of the time in the mirror, my stomach rises like a swell of ocean waves. This is it–a real date.

I'm not just hanging out with Cally's family or a group of friends from around town that happens to have a few guys in it. I'm going out, on purpose, with a guy. It'll be just him and me. It's my first real date in almost three years. I suppose I've been busier than I'd like to admit. Maybe I'm the go-getter who needs to relax more instead of Lukas.

No, he definitely wins the prize there.

The sound of the doorbell echoes through my apartment, and I swallow hard. I'm excited, sure, but how can a girl not be a little bit nervous when she hasn't been on a date in so long?

I take a deep breath and head downstairs to open the back door of my aunt's shop. Before opening it, I take a deep breath in and let it out as slowly as I can manage. It comes out a little stuttery, but when my lungs are depleted, I twist the knob and pull.

"Autumn," Lukas says, smoothly and confidently.

"Hi," I reply sheepishly in return.

He is dressed in the suit from the first time I laid eyes on him, the charcoal gray one. He's ditched the blue diamond tie, probably in an effort to "relax." Honestly, the slightly opened white collared shirt underneath is doing a lot for him.

"Your aunt showed me back here. I would have texted you but… somehow I walked away from you without getting your number last time," Lukas says smoothly.

My first thought is, "Oh, no, he met Aunt Bev already?" The second is, "Why did I not get his number that night?" And third, "Why don't you wipe off that drool and try producing some words, Autumn?"

But I don't have time to kick myself. "I'm glad you made it," I manage to say, opening the door up a bit wider. "I came down without my purse, so why don't you come up for a second?"

Lukas steps through the threshold and starts up the stairs behind me.

"You're very punctual." Maybe it's a silly way to break the awkward silence, but it's what comes out. "It's exactly five o'clock."

Lukas pushes the door closed behind him and watches me cross the living room. He glances around curiously as he answers. "I make it a point to always be on time."

"That must present a challenge in New York," I say. "Isn't there a lot of traffic?"

"I'm always up to the challenge," he tells me.

"That's something I can tell about you," I say. "I'll just grab my bag and finish getting ready. Just make yourself comfortable. I'll only be a couple of minutes."

Before I can start feeling too giddy about the handsome man in my living room, I spin around into my bedroom and shut the door. He's only been here for three minutes! "Get ahold of yourself, girl!" I whisper to myself through clenched teeth.

I check myself in my mirror and add a couple of waves to my hair. I slide on another layer of deodorant, just to be sure, then apply a final touch of lip tint. I snag my purse off the sun-shaped wall hook and talk myself through another deep breath before opening the door.

I spot Lukas strolling through my front room.

"I like your place," he says without turning around.

The edge of the room, which marks the halfway point between my bedroom door and the front door, seems like the most natural place to stand, so I park myself there.

"It's no New York penthouse," I say. "But I guess it's not too bad."

He peeks over his shoulder, wearing a dashing smile that literally makes my knees forget their job. "This is more charming." He says it so simply, so easily. I believe him right away.

I watch as Lukas walks over to my bookshelf and runs his finger along the spines. He leans in slightly to study a photo of my mother and me sitting on a picnic blanket in the middle of the apple orchard. I was about seven in the photo and have two little braided pigtails. Next thing I know, I'm standing right next to him, leaning in slightly to look at the picture, too.

"Your hair got redder," he notes. There is a little glimmer of light in his eyes that makes my heart feel like it's being lifted off the ground by a hot-air balloon.

I subconsciously touch my hair, which has definitely grown more strawberry these fifteen years later. I don't stop him from looking at my belongings. In fact, I rather like that he's taken an interest in my home.

"So I guess this place is a lot different from your house, huh?" I ask, crossing my arms loosely. "Was I far off on the penthouse comment?"

Lukas turns to look at me over his shoulder again. He presses his lips together slightly and sighs softly out of his nose. "I like it," he says. "Your house. It feels like a home, like someone lives here."

I think the observation is a little amusing and obvious, so I can't help but let out a little laugh. "Well, someone does live here. Me."

He returns my laugh with a light chuckle of his own. "Obviously," he says, turning to look at me head on. I'm suddenly very conscious of how he's gazing at me, and I grip onto my elbows as if I can steady myself that way. I want to look away because this is all so unfamiliar, but I can't bring myself to break our gaze.

"Obviously you live here," he says, studying me. "I just mean that it's warm and inviting."

"Then, what's your house like?" I ask, shifting forward. I don't recall moving so close to him, but now we're a mere footstep apart.

Lukas sucks in a breath that seems to hold a lot of weight. He holds it for a second and then lets it go silently. I see his shoulders drop slightly with the release, but I wonder how much tension he's still holding onto in there. It makes me want to reach out and touch him.

I squeeze my elbows tighter.

"Honestly, my house is cold. I'm not even sure I have more than chicken breast and water in the fridge. I hire someone to clean the place every week, but they don't have to do a lot because I'm hardly there to make a mess. I wouldn't call it a home. It's just… where I live."

That sounds sad to me. I want to know more about Lukas. I wonder why he works so much. I want to get a feel for the kind of person he is outside of his perfectly tailored suit and styled hair. But all I can do is hope that he'll decide to share it with me when he's ready.

❧

LUKAS IS STANDING IN FRONT OF THE NEWEST DISPLAY OF MEN'S
sweaters at the department store. I'm sure it's much different from
shopping in New York. We don't have all the expensive, name brand
places here. But Lukas doesn't seem to mind. Apparently, after getting
fitted once, he just orders his suits online.

"You really don't know yourself, do you?" I ask a little quietly. "We
just need to find something that's comfortable to wear."

"Corporate life doesn't call for comfort, so yes, I'll need to adjust."
He seems a little disappointed that I haven't approved of the last three
sweaters he's tried to pick out.

I rummage through the rack of new arrivals and grab two options.
I walk them around the table and press them into his arms. "I bet you
don't even have a winter scarf, do you?"

He shifts his gaze, and that is all the evidence I need that the
answer is yes.

"What do you think of these two?" I ask him, gesturing at the two
sweaters I've piled in his hands. One is gray, like the suit. And even as
he holds it, I can tell it'll bring out the depth of his eyes. And the other
is a creamy off-white cable-knit.

"Are you sure?" he asks, holding up the cable knit one. "White? I'm
usually a black and gray kind of guy."

I shrug. "It's just a suggestion," I say. "I just think it'll look good on
you. And this off-white, creamy color is the perfect balance between
warm, relaxing, and stylish."

A soft smile twitches at the corner of his mouth. "Okay, then. Pick
out a couple more. Since I don't seem to have my sense of casual style,
let's see what you think of me."

The way he says it makes my stomach flutter. What I think of
him....

It's hard to say, being that this is only our second day having a conversation, but already I can tell that he is sincere. He might be a level of polished that I don't understand, but I also see that as a sense of pride, not in a cocky way, but in a confident way. He seems curious, but guarded, meticulous, but maybe a little worn down by plans he's made for himself.

About an hour later, I've examined the rest of the store, including the clearance section—I'm not above saving money, even when it's his. Lukas trails right behind me as I go along, piling clothes into his arms. He graciously goes through them and selects several he's willing to try, and he even chooses a few pairs of jeans. To my surprise, he wears the off-white cable-knit sweater and a pair of jeans that have no business looking that good on anyone out of the store.

"I'm ready," he says, with two bags full of other clothes in his other hand. "Let's go on our date."

My heart nearly thumps out of my ribcage. Our date....

I drive us across town to Cally's family restaurant, Maple Falls Café, telling him some facts about the town and its landmarks and people. He teases me for sounding like a tour guide again. After the shopping, things feel easy between us, playful. And I like the way his laugh sounds in every variety.

At the restaurant, we're seated in a cozy booth with string lights overhead, but we're surrounded by lots of families with little kids that are a bit noisy. It might not be the ideal place for a romantic date, but the point is to get Lukas to relax. We only say sorry the first two times our knees bump together, but after that, they just seem to keep finding each other. Our eyes do the same, locking together and then roaming freely over the other person's features. Neither of us try to hide.

We're interrupted a couple of times by passersby who I know, but it doesn't ruin the moment. I don't think anything can. I just say hi to them, and Lukas introduces himself naturally, then we get back to our little section of the world where only the two of us exist.

"This place reminds me of home," Lukas tells me.

"Home? New York?"

He shakes his head. "Nebraska."

My jaw drops. "You're a Midwesterner?!"

Lukas chuckles and nods. "That's right."

"You fooled me," I say with mock betrayal.

Lukas grows a little quiet, but he still wears a soft smile.

Without thinking, I reach across and tap him on the hand with my finger. "Tell me about your home," I say.

CHAPTER 10

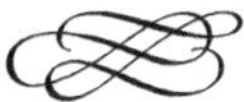

Between sets on the bench press and cable machine, I think about our night together. Our initial meeting had been an endearing kind of awkward, but we quickly found our groove. I should have known after our first night meeting in the woods that Autumn was intriguing. She proved to be ever clever and lighthearted. I had to keep restraining myself from the desire to hold her hand or just touch her, but I delighted in every moment we made contact, be it an accidental brush or a gentle, purposeful touch on the arm.

For the first time in many years, I talked to someone about my home, about Nebraska. And I didn't talk about it regretfully. Sure, thinking about my parents and home had weight, and maybe a touch of heartache that I couldn't quite identify, but mostly it felt nostalgic.

I told her about climbing hay bales and splashing in the creek with my old friend Timothy. I told her about catching big ol' bullfrogs and taking long drives with no houses in sight, about the breathtaking sunsets and the way the ground got all crisped up and hard in the heat of the summer. I talked about making tater tot casserole with my mom and learning how to drive from my dad.

By the end of the night, some of the weight had been replaced by a sense of longing to reconnect, to ease up. I'm so far apart from what my life used to be.

Autumn, after just two days, has changed my mindset so much. Four hours with her isn't enough. It's too bad that she has to work today because I could have kept up our conversation all night and into today. Instead, I'm stuck just thinking about it, working out in what turns out is a fairly decent gym in the inn. Branden doesn't have anything planned for us, so I'm free to do whatever I want to all day. But all I want is to be in Autumn's presence again, to pick up where we left off when I dropped her off at home.

After about an hour of weights, I decide to tack on a run, and on my way back, Ivy stops me in the middle of the front lawn. "Taking advantage of this beautiful morning, I see," she says cheerily. She has a nice, kind smile.

I stop a few feet away from her and wipe the sweat off my brow with the shoulder of my T-shirt. "It was nice," I admit. The sun has gradually grown brighter as the morning mist drops away and gives way to the light.

"What else do you have planned today?" Ivy asks.

I shrug. "Honestly, I haven't thought that far ahead."

She studies me for a moment and shifts on her feet. "I'm not sure if it's your style, but there is a pottery workshop taking place over in the event space. You might check it out if it piques your interest."

My instinct is to laugh and brush it off. Pottery? Normally, I'd say it's a waste of time. But then I think about how it might be nice to use my hands for something other than typing out texts and emails.

"Okay," I say. "I might check it out."

It seems like she's about to leave. "Oh, is there anything you need? There've been a lot of complaints about the spotty cell service. I hope it's not inconveniencing you too much."

I just wave her off. "That's all right. It's supposed to be a break, after all. At least that's what people keep telling me."

Ivy shares one more pleasant smile before telling me to enjoy the day and skipping off into the inn.

I pull my phone out of my pocket, checking first for any sign of a response from Autumn and then looking at my emails.

"There you are!" A high-pitched voice pierces through the air. "I went to your room, but you weren't there!"

I sigh and turn to face Julia. Between Branden's little team activities and being stuck in the same not-big-enough inn, I've been seeing a lot of Julia, more than when we were at the office, anyway.

"I was just taking a run," I say, moving up the steps.

She puts her hand on my chest to stop me, but quickly shakes it off. "You're all sweaty." Her nose scrunches up, and she wipes her hands on her skirt.

I just shrug and shake it off, pushing her hand away. Perhaps it's laced with insolence, but Julia's reaction is priceless. She gasps and jumps back, acting as though some of my sweat actually landed on her arm. It was nowhere near her.

"Ugh! Lukas!" she says with a stomp. "That's so gross."

I walk past her again, but I feel her following close behind me, so I stop. "What, Julia? I just want to take a shower. What do you want?"

A sly little smile streaks across her face, but I don't have time for her flirty nonsense. I turn around. "Why are you being so mean to me?" she whines.

"I'm not being mean," I say without breaking a step. "I'm just going to my room. You said it yourself. I'm gross."

She huffs, hot on my heels. "That's not what I mean. You have hardly talked to me this whole trip!"

"I think I've talked to you a normal amount."

"No," she says flatly. "You haven't. You're ignoring me."

I take a hint and halt. She bumps into my sweaty back, and for once, she takes a step away. She clearly isn't going to let me get away without telling her what she wants to hear. I look at her, waiting.

"Can't you just have lunch with me?" she asks.

"I'm doing a thing later. I won't be around at lunchtime."

"Dinner then?"

I shake my head. "Hanging with Thomas."

Julia's face is slowly becoming cherry-like in redness, her eyes piercing. "Another time then," she tells me rather than asks, and she crosses her arms.

I'm not sure why she's insisting so hard, but I concede. "Sure, fine. Some other time."

She presses her lips together and nods with finality.

THOUGH IT HAD ORIGINALLY BEEN A STRETCH OF THE TRUTH, I convince Thomas to have dinner with me. After a surprisingly difficult and equally surprisingly fun time at the pottery workshop—which I learned was a weekly ordeal—I made sure that he was free. I wanted to talk about my date with Autumn.

"What are you eating?" Thomas asks now, sliding up to one of the smaller dining tables at the inn. He looks rather relaxed in gray sweats and a plain white tee. His dark blond stubble is even coming in, giving off a hipster vibe.

"I was waiting for you."

Thomas grins at me, and we go get our dinner from the buffet in the dining room. I wave to Luis on my way by with a full plate. It's heaped up with mashed potatoes, roasted asparagus, beef tips, and baked chicken breast garnished with a slice of lemon. Of the many things they do well here, cooking is the one I appreciate most.

"Looks like you're settling in nicely," I tell Thomas, gesturing to his ensemble.

He simply laughs and shoves a heaping spoonful of mystery casserole into his mouth. After he swallows, he gestures back at me. "What about you? You went on a little shopping spree or something? Don't think I didn't notice this little number you've got on."

The 'little number' is the gray sweater and pair of dark wash jeans that Autumn picked out. She'd given me some tips on how to make the look casual versus dressed up, and I'd found myself wanting to experience the same kind of ease and relaxation that she told me I should try. I have to admit, I like the way it looks and the way it feels. It's not so… limiting.

"Yeah, actually, I did go on a shopping spree," I admit. "And I wasn't alone."

Thomas stops another spoonful of casserole just centimeters away from his mouth. He places the silverware back on his plate slowly and clasps his hands like he's about to take part in a fascinating press conference. "I'm sorry. Can you say that again? You weren't alone?"

I roll my eyes. "Is it so hard to believe that I went out with someone?"

Suddenly, Thomas snaps to attention. He's looking over my shoulder like he's seeing the ghost of some long-dead celebrity. "Wait, it wasn't Julia, right?" he whispers.

Just as I'm turning my head to answer, a hand lands on my shoulder, and along with it, the familiar stench of Julia's rose perfume. "Hey, handsome," she says. "I guess you really are eating dinner with Thomas. I thought you were just blowing me off."

The muscles in my chest and shoulders tighten. So much for relaxing and reminiscing about yesterday.

"I'll go grab a small plate and join you!" she cheers.

Before either of us says anything, Julia is teetering away on her red-bottomed stilettos.

"If it wasn't Julia, then who was it?" Thomas asks right away.

With Julia gone and the topic of conversation switched back to Autumn, my shoulders release. "Autumn."

He doesn't seem to recall her, as unfathomable as that is to me. "She was on the tour bus. I ran into her that one night."

His eyes wide with recollection, Thomas's mouth drops open slightly. "No way! She's pretty hot!"

I feel a bit of heat prickling the back of my neck and ears. "Yeah. And she's so fun. I don't know how to explain it, but the way she just goes with the flow and finds the simple things so enjoyable is really admirable. And her laugh is incredible. Oh, and when she's annoyed—

but you know, in an amused way—she purses her lips together and stares at me like—"

"You're so smitten already," Thomas teases.

I scoff and shake my head. "I don't know if I'd say smitten, but, yes, I like her."

Thomas gives me a strange look and gives a doubtful sort of frown. "This should be interesting then," he whispers as the stilettos return.

Julia slides into the seat next to me and pats my knee. Instinctively, I shift myself away. Ever since that night three years ago when I agreed to dance with her at a company function, she's been a different kind of comfortable around me. I wasn't sure how to take it after all of this time, but now it's starting to make me uncomfortable.

"What're you two talking about? Looks like you made Lukey here all shy," she says, pinching my cheeks lightly.

"It's nothing," I say, taking a bite of food. It's pretty tasty. The beef tips are cooked perfectly, juicy and light in the center.

Julia's "small plate" is filled with leaf lettuce and tomatoes. There's not even dressing.

"Is that all you're eating?" I ask. "You're going to pass out from malnutrition someday."

Julia rolls her eyes but quickly changes gears and bats her eyelashes at me instead. "Aw, are you worried about me, Lukey?"

"I've asked you not to use that nickname."

She doesn't seem to acknowledge that and instead changes the subject. More complaints about Vermont and having nothing to do. More comments on this "shabby little inn" and "shabby little people."

It only takes a couple of minutes before I can't take it anymore. Thomas is nodding along absentmindedly.

"You're not even trying to like this place," I blurt out.

Julia seems legitimately stunned by my statement. "Excuse me?"

"I'm just saying," I check my tone, reining in the explosiveness that erupted for a split second. "Why don't you go into town, park yourself in a little coffee shop or a wine bar, and just live in the moment? It's not as bad as you're making it out to be."

If I were ready to be honest with myself, I'd acknowledge where my sudden defensiveness about this town is coming from. But I just cross my arms and look at Thomas for help.

He clears his throat, unsure.

"What are you talking about?" Julia asks, turning to face me. "I thought you hated this place as much as me. It's no secret you weren't looking forward to coming here."

I keep my eyes trained on Thomas, who is looking at me with confusion and concern. "Well, things have changed," I say matter-of-factly.

"Because of a girl?" she asks.

I don't answer. After a couple more minutes of Julia poking at her flavorless lettuce and sulking about me raising my voice at her, she excuses herself.

"Seems like Julia is jealous," Thomas mutters around a mouthful of potatoes.

I scoff. "Why would she be jealous? It's not like we ever dated."

"That doesn't mean she doesn't want to."

"No way," I say. I take the last bite of mashed potatoes. "She complains too much. And I can't deal with someone that high-maintenance."

Thomas nods in agreement. "So, about this Autumn girl…Are you going to ask her out again? It seems like you're pretty invested."

"I'd like to," I admit.

We chat a little longer about the date, and Thomas tells me he's never lounged in bed so long and that he might make it his new office.

After dinner, I start heading up to my room. But I stop at the stairwell when I see Julia standing at the top. It's a little too obvious that she's waiting for me, and the angry look on her face doesn't give me the strongest desire to confront her.

We make eye contact, but I think of a better idea. I spin on my heels and head out the door.

It's time to see if this town has Uber.

CHAPTER 11

I meet Cally for lunch when the sudden rush of customers at Blue Kiss dies down. It's nearly an hour later than I intended to go eat, and I'm hungry! Thankfully, Cally's family restaurant, Maple Falls Cafe, is close by. I was just here the night before with Lukas, and the vibe is totally different now. In the bright peak of the day there's still several families here, but their volume is muted, and the twinkle lights aren't shining in the window. The counter area is empty save for one middle-aged man with long, curly gray hair cascading from underneath his ball-cap. Inside, the twinkling lights are also off, and instead, the room is filled with the soft glow of daylight. It still feels homey and familiar to me, but it's a drastic change from last night.

"Spill it," Cally says even before I have time to sit down. "I wanna hear every detail. Every."

I plop my purse into the booth, which is directly across the room from where Lukas and I had dined, and slide in. Cally is trembling with giddiness and watching me with an expectant smile.

"Well?" she probes.

I pick up a menu, pretending like I don't already know what I want even though I always get it, and acting like I'm not devastatingly thrilled to talk about my date with Lukas. Playing the stubborn, teasing game seems like a good move until Cally's excitement gets to me.

When Jarred, our usual day waiter, brings me water with lemon and lime slices, and walks away, I take a sip and let my excitement out, too.

"Oh, my gosh, I had such a good time I don't even know where to start," I blurt out, the sentence practically blurring into a single word.

A creepy, impish smile takes over Cally's face. "I knew it."

I roll my eyes. "You did not." She totally did.

Squeezing my lemon and then my lime into my water, I think about where I should begin. This time, Cally waits semi-patiently for me to start.

"First," I begin, "he is so, so cute. Underneath that stony businessman demeanor, he's actually a very nice guy. And he's also a little flirty. I think he's totally out of his realm here in this little town, which is a little weird considering he's from Nebraska."

Cally startles. "Wait, what? Like Omaha, Nebraska, or cornfields and cows, Nebraska?"

A little chuckle escapes me because I was surprised when I'd first heard that as well. "His family owns a farm. They've had it for over forty years, or something like that. I guess his mom and dad started it."

"I never would have guessed that," Cally says, disbelief audible in her voice. "So, how'd he end up in New York?"

"He hasn't really shared those details with me yet," I explain. "We talked about his life before New York and his life now, but I still don't know what happened in between. I think he was just looking for success, for something different."

Cally gazes off thoughtfully. "Interesting. See, I only saw him like two times, but he sure seemed different last night."

I almost choke on my water. "What? You saw him last night?"

She just grins and wiggles her eyebrows. "I have eyes everywhere," she says, wiggling her fingers in the air around us. "He looked pretty cozy."

Of course, she would have found a way to spy on my first date in years. How embarrassing.

"We actually went shopping for those clothes. It was so funny." Another laugh escapes me as I think about how surprisingly hopeless he looked while attempting to pick out sweaters. "He was trying to find clothes, but everything he chose was so... odd. He obviously has great taste in suits. But when it comes to casual clothes, he was clueless in the cutest way."

"That is cute," Cally says, "but that's not what I'm talking about. I mean, he looked cozy with you."

My heart hops, skips, and skids. I mean, I felt that sort of comfort with him last night, but part of me wondered if it was just in my head. Maybe I'd created some sort of dreamlike fantasy that night because of all the romance novels I've been reading. I'm not sure I totally trust myself. It's just been so long since I had a real date, I wasn't sure whether I was thinking clearly or if I'd been carried off by my hummingbird heart.

But if even Cally thinks we looked "cozy" together, then maybe it was real after all.

"Look at you and your cute little blush," Cally says, pointing to my face.

"Maybe we flirted a little," I admit. "And maybe we connected in a way that was unexpected."

Cally chatters out another laugh reminiscent of a capuchin. "Connected? Tell me more. What do you think of him? Really."

As if I could lie....

"He's interesting and refreshing," I tell her. "He's different in a sense I don't really understand. And... something about him tells me that he's itching to let his guard down."

"Are you sure?" Cally asks. "He just seemed so–"

She hooks her arms in two right angles and moves them robotically. I give her my best deadpan stare, but a smirk wins over.

"Really," she says. "He looks all business. And I bet he works like a hundred hours a week."

My face falls. "I think he actually does."

My best friend looks at me quizzically.

"When we talked about New York, he couldn't tell me anything," I add, "not even his favorite restaurant. I don't think he's done a single touristy thing since he's been there, and he doesn't seem to know what the locals do there, either. I think he literally just works and works, and that he's been doing nothing but that since he moved there."

"Oh, yeah, I'm sure that's the case."

Now that I'm talking about him working all the time, I'm momentarily distracted with thoughts of the way his suit tugs against his broad shoulders.

"And he's not bad to look at, either," she blurts.

The blush rises hotter on my cheeks.

I scold her by stealing one of her curly fries. Then, between bites of sloppy joe and sips of our sodas, Cally and I sit and talk about the date, up to the sweet moment when Lukas walked me to the outside door of my apartment and instead of going in for a hug or a kiss, just grazed my arm in a simple way that left it tingling until I fell asleep. I told her about the way he smiled with his lips pressed together as he watched me step safely inside the corridor, and the way he said goodbye so softly that it melted into my skin, and seems to still be lingering there....

"He sounds like a gentleman, at least," Cally says. She seems genuinely impressed, and that makes me feel glad, like she's validating that I'm not crazy to be attracted to Lukas and that it might be reasonable for me to have a massive girlish crush on him after meeting him only a couple of times. "Are you going to go out again?" she asks.

I shrug. "I'd like to." I tuck a wild auburn strand of hair behind my ear. "But I guess we'll see."

"You're not going to ask him out?" She seems dumbfounded, her mouth agape and everything.

I snort. "Why would I ask him out? If he's interested, he'll ask me, right?"

Cally narrows her eyes at me. "Yeah, I guess so."

AUNT BEVERLY IS IN ONE OF HER RARE QUIET AND DETACHED MOODS. After closing up the shop for the day and cleaning for twenty minutes in complete silence, I break the tension lingering in the air. "It's tomorrow, right?" I ask. "His birthday?"

She gives me a gentle nod of her head.

Without a word, I move across the few feet between us and envelop her in a hug. She drops the broom she's sweeping with and wraps her arms around me. For a couple of minutes, she cries softly on my shoulder. I feel the warm moisture seeping through the open knit of my cardigan.

"Sorry," she says after sniffling. She breaks away from me gently and wipes her eyes. "Just when I think it's getting easier, it rips me open again."

I can't even imagine the pain she must feel daily. "There's no need to apologize," I tell her.

She picks up the broom and starts sweeping again, but I take it out of her hands.

"Why don't we do something together tomorrow?" I suggest.

She gives a sad smile. "That's sweet, Autumn, but I just want to spend tomorrow with him. I think there's a Lake Monsters game. He loved…." She drifts off. "Anyway, I think I'll just wear his favorite jersey and hat, visit the Kissing Bridge, then catch the game. I'll order a late night pizza and rewatch the game on TV."

For nearly ten years she's been without him, and she's still so heartbroken. It breaks my heart to see her hurting. Sometimes I want to ask her if she thinks she'll ever be able to move on, but I can't bring myself to say the words. So I let her be, as usual, letting her do what she thinks she needs to do and just waiting to see if she reaches out.

We finish tidying up the shop and settle the register. Before we push out the back door, she grabs my wrist lightly. "Maybe tonight?"

"Huh?"

"Tonight. We can watch a movie or something? You can bring Tess. She'd love to run around the backyard, I'm sure."

I nod. "Yeah."

"Just, uh, give me like an hour to pull myself together," she says.

I shake my head and give her a warm smile. "You don't have to pull yourself together around me, but I'll give you the time you need."

"One hour," she suggests again. "One hour and no more because I don't know if I can—"

I squeeze her hand. "I'll be there."

Aunt Bev pushes the door open and immediately stops in her tracks. "Well, hello there," she says in her usual strong, cheery voice.

I peek around her and almost topple to the ground when I trip over the back of her heel. Strong hands grab me by the elbows. I look up into the warm pools of Lukas's eyes, speechless.

"Is falling in my presence a habit of yours?" he asks smoothly.

My stomach dips, but I'm quickly brought back to reality by my aunt's snicker.

"Hardly," I say, straightening out the hem of my cardigan that got looped over my arm in the jumble. "You just happened to catch me on the two rare occasions."

His smile is blazing, breathtaking, bewitching. I think I feel my spirit actually leave my body when he teases me, "And it's a good thing I did, too."

In the corner of my eye, I see Aunt Bev curl her lips in to hide a smile. "Anyway," she chirps, "I'll see you later... or...?"

It's tempting to assume that Lukas is here to ask me out again, but I can't just leave my aunt on a night like tonight, especially not after she cried in my arms and asked me to be with her. "I'll be there," I reassure her.

She pardons herself, leaving Lukas and me alone together in the space between the shop and the building located behind us. I watch her back out and drive away, and when I look back at Lukas, he's watching me.

"What?" I ask, suddenly self-conscious. I tuck my hair behind my ear and my cheeks start to heat.

"Let's go on another date."

I'm struck by the lack of hesitation in his voice.

"Sorry?" Surely I misheard him.

Lukas chuckles and takes a step to close the already minimal space between us. If it weren't for the bit of September breeze blowing between us, I might have been able to feel his breath reach my already warm cheeks. "I want to go on another date with you."

Now, it's my turn to pull in my lips to fight a smile. "Is that right?" Can't you think of something better to say, Autumn?

"It seems like you already have plans tonight," he says. "But that just means I have more time to plan something... say... tomorrow? You don't have to work, right?"

I shake my head.

"To clarify, is that a no to the date, or no to tomorrow or no to having to work?" he asks, without a hint of wavering in his voice.

"I'm excited to see what you think up," I tell him. "I'd like to find out whether 'Mister Never Leaves His Office and is Suddenly Left With an Abundance of Free Time in Unfamiliar Territory' has decent planning skills."

There's that breathtaking smile again. I touch my chest to make sure my heart is beating.

"I won't disappoint you," he says.

WHEN I STEP INSIDE MY AUNT'S HOUSE, I LET TESS RUN FREE. AS SOON as I walk into the same room as my aunt, she's practically wearing heart eyes. "If that's not the start of love, I don't know what is!" she screeches.

I laugh, blushing so hard I feel the heat all the way from my neck to my forehead. "We'll see," I tell her. "But it's far too soon to talk about the magic of love just yet."

CHAPTER 12

I loved Autumn's reaction when I asked her out again last night, and she's doing it again right now in the passenger seat with her hands clasped nervously together between her knees. She looks out the window, her gaze fixed with a mix of wonder and apprehension. This is the first time I've seen this kind of look on her face. There's so much about her I don't know yet.

I believe I'm curious to find out.

"You scared of my driving?" I tease her. It takes everything in me not to reach over and envelop her hands in mine. ,To keep myself from holding them, rubbing little reassuring circles over her knuckles. But it's only our second date, and I only picked her up a few minutes ago.

She flips a menacing yet endearing glare my way. "I'll have you know that I don't normally let strangers drag me along to undisclosed locations very often."

I'm beginning to like it when she gets quippy. "I thought we moved past the 'stranger' phase that night with the near-bear attack."

She scrunches her nose to contain a smile, but I see it in her eyes, her beautiful, illuminating green eyes. "Eyes on the road, friend."

Even though she calls me 'friend' I doubt either of us sees the other that way. I reluctantly fix my eyes back on the road. It had rained earlier in the morning, and now the roads are glittering with rainwater. The sky is slate blue with low-hanging clouds. It's the kind of quiet, peaceful morning reminiscent of the time my father would drag me out of bed at five A.M. for morning chores, and a couple of hours later, when the sky was lit up like this, the moisture of the night still lingering in the air. It felt freeing. I wonder where I lost the ability to enjoy that.

"I thought dates weren't for 'friends'?" I ask.

"Okay, then, TBD." Her voice is airy and liberating, like coming out of the office after a twelve-hour day and loosening up my muscles with a run. No, it's even better than that.

I can't help but smirk. "It's not the best nickname, but I'll take it for now," I say.

A moment of silence passes before Autumn speaks up again. "Now, I know we're going to some fancy-smancy place, but just how far away is it?"

I explain that it's just a twenty-minute drive to the next town over, the slightly larger city of Grant, hence the Lexus I'd rented. I wanted to lead this date, to ensure we'd have our own way to get around and didn't have to depend on an Uber. So, I spent the whole night planning it. I just hope she enjoys it as much as I will.

Fifteen minutes and some small talk about hobbies later, we pull into a space outside of the restaurant I'd chosen, Cascade. I told Autumn beforehand it was a place to dress up. And, boy, did she. She looks incredible in an emerald fitted dress with long sleeves. In her blocky heels, she's just a few inches shorter than me, and when she stands next to me, her face is closer and I can get a better look at her eyes. Man, a couple of inches makes a world of difference.

I offer her my arm, and she giggles before taking it. "My friend would instantly fall in love with you if you pulled this move on her."

"I'm sure your friend is great," I say, "but this 'move' is all yours."

She quickly looks away from me, but not before I see her smile. "Wow," she says quietly. She looks around the place in wonder. "How did you find this place?"

"It's the power of intermittent Wi-Fi," I explain.

Cascade is a slightly upscale brunch place. It's currently decked out in a fall theme, with glittery leaves woven through the wooden rafters and glowing lanterns hanging from the ceiling. The slightly gray day outside makes the inside feel even more cozy and bright.

I hold Autumn's purse and help her remove her jacket as we make ourselves comfortable at our reserved table. It's an intimate setting at a round table with a white linen tablecloth and a couple of pink and yellow candles burning in the center.

"So, you like this place?" I ask.

She's still looking around at the decor with the gold-lined menu loose in her hands. "It's so pretty," she says with a soft smile.

Her smile makes me send one back to her. "I'm glad."

"You know," she says, finally looking at me again. Her eyes have taken on that radiant glow again that seems to mesmerize me. "Aside from trips with my parents, I haven't taken the initiative to do any exploring on my own outside of Maple Falls. Who knew a beautiful place like this was so close by?"

We share a smile and a long gaze. It feels like we're the only people here.

"And who knew someone who has lived in New York his whole life but can't tell me the name of the next street over found it all on his own," she adds, shaking her head with mock smugness.

"I have my moments," I reply, "especially when I need to impress someone as beautiful as you."

Her face falls for a second and then glows pink.

I rest my forearms on the table, amused. "Tell me, Autumn, are you not used to men flirting with you?"

She slowly raises the menu in front of her, hiding, I'm sure, her burning red face. "No," she mutters quietly.

I place a hand gently on her menu and press down until I see her.

She avoids my eyes, but I'm right. Her face and neck are pink, like a summer sunrise.

"Now, then, are the men of Maple Falls blind, or just dumb?"

She lowers her face even more. "I don't know. Both?"

This elicits a hearty laugh out of me.

"I believe most of the appropriately aged men are married," she says in a sheepish voice.

Maybe shy Autumn was winning over quippy Autumn now, so I back off to make her more comfortable again. I want her to enjoy the evening.

"This food sounds great," I say to change the subject, looking over my menu.

"It does," she agrees.

The waitress comes over, and we give her our order. While we're waiting for the food, Autumn tells me a little bit about her aunt and what today meant to her. It's sad to hear about her Uncle Henry's death. The way she speaks about the sort of beautiful, pure marriage he and her Aunt Beverly had leaves a lump in my throat.

"If we need to go back at any time, just say the word," I tell her.

Her eyes are getting a little red-rimmed, but she blinks it away and shakes her head. "Thank you. Anyway, let's change the subject before I cry off my mascara."

It's funny. Julia could have said something similar, but it would have sounded so different.

"So… what are your career plans?" I ask to change the subject again.

"That sounds like an interview question," she teases me.

"Maybe," I agree. "But I want to know more about you."

She grins. "All right. To answer your question, I'd love to just do tours forever."

Her answer is too simple. I feel like there's something missing. "And…?"

Her resolve breaks just enough. "I guess… if the opportunity were ever to present itself, I would love to take over the tour operation."

I nod, encouraging her to keep going. I want to hear it all.

"Well," she begins again with slight hesitation. "Mr. Seeley is getting older. I know he's thinking of retiring. Not a lot of people know that the company is already up for sale, but there haven't been any offers, anyway."

"What's stopping you?" I ask.

She shrugs. "I certainly can't afford it."

"Even when you've been working two jobs?"

She explains that her aunt's place pays decently because it's doing well and she's the primary employee other than her aunt. The tours are low paying, just minimum wage, but she does it because she loves it. I can't imagine working so many hours for so little, but somehow with Autumn, it makes sense. She has the perfect mindset–pleased easily by little things, not caring too much about things that don't hold any weight. Even during the tours, before I actually knew her, I could tell that she really loves her work.

After we get our food, it's my turn to be in the hot seat. She asks about how I got into financial management and advising. I admit that it was a whole whirlwind of choices falling like dominoes that landed me there. And that's the bulk of the truth.

"So, do you like your job? Are you satisfied with it?" she asks.

Am I satisfied? I haven't asked myself that before. I'm always working toward a short-term goal, always trying to meet the next deadline, to make the numbers bigger. My goal has always been success, but what does that even mean? How do I measure it? How do I know when I have achieved it?

I finally answer her honestly. "I don't know."

She accepts my answer with poise and doesn't push much more. Part of me wishes she would. It feels like she is slowly cracking me open from some kind of shell I didn't even realize I had been trapped in.

We finish our food and take a walk outside instead of getting right back in the car. We stroll silently alongside one another, our shoulders brushing occasionally, both our hands in our pockets. I imagine that it's uncomfortable to walk in those heels for long, so I suggest we take a seat on a nearby bench that overlooks a man-made lake. There are a few waterfowl swimming around, ducking their heads into the water. Autumn laughs at the way their feet kick around in the air, and I laugh alongside her.

She points out a little brown and white dachshund jogging alongside a man and tells me that it looks like Tess, her dog. We talk for a moment about dog versus cat people. She mocks surprise when I tell her I used to sneak the barn cats into my room when I was little, but I've always liked dogs, too.

A little while later, although its rays aren't particularly warm, the sun has come out. I appreciate the way its light shines through the multicolored leaves and makes little dappled spots in the grass. The air is still cool and damp from an earlier shower, and I like the way the air feels weighty and refreshing.

Autumn sighs and tilts her head back, letting the sun wash over her face. She closes her eyes and takes a deep breath. Without thinking about it, I follow suit. Fall is beautiful, and it turns out it's worth simply acknowledging that.

I would have forgotten that if not for her.

CHAPTER 13

It dawns on me suddenly as I'm looking at Lukas with his head tilted back and his eyes closed. I like this version of him, but how long is it going to last? I was having such a wonderful time with him that I haven't stopped to think about reality. And reality says that he lives in New York. He'll only be here for a month—slightly less than that now. He is going to go back to his do-nothing-but-work life in the city. Which means he'll move past this blip in his life.

"Lukas," I say, feeling more nervous than I have been.

His eyes open slowly, and with his head still reclined, he glances over at me. His eyes are a little heavy, and I see the faintest upward tuck at the corners of his mouth. "Yes, Autumn?"

"Are you excited to go back home? To New York, I mean." I have this strange tightness in my chest. Anxiety?

His Adam's apple bobs up and down before he answers. "Yeah," he says. "I'm ready to get back to work. A man can only take so much time off when he's lived in his office for ten years. I think I'm going through withdrawal."

I laugh, but it feels shallow.

"But I've had a lot of fun here, especially with you," he adds.

My heart wants to be giddy, but my chest just tightens even more. Suddenly I want to move, to head back home. I stand, surprising Lukas out of his relaxation. "I hate to cut this day short if you had more planned," I tell him. "But I think I'd like to go back home. You know... my Aunt Bev...."

Lukas stands and studies my face. "Okay," he says. "That's fine. Let's get you back then."

In the car on the way back, he talks about some of the other places he found while he was looking for places to visit today, but I have a hard time focusing on the conversation. My mind is a torrent of thoughts, trying to decipher what he meant when he said he was excited to go back but how he also has been having a good time here. It's confusing.

Am I just a fun, brief reprieve from his busy life? I wonder. Does he just see me as a way to pass the time in this little town in the middle of nowhere until he can get back to his real life?

Once again, Lukas walks me to the back door of the shop.

"I hope you had fun today," he says, and he sounds sincere, as far as I can tell.

I give him a smile that feels half-hearted. "I did." I don't want him to think... well... that I'm upset, so I add on, "Cascade is a really pretty place. And the food was fantastic. Thank you for taking me there."

Lukas cocks his head slightly. I feel behind me for the doorknob and twist. "I'll see you again?" he asks.

My stomach feels tighter now. The longer I'm in Lukas's presence, the more I wonder about what he said or what he might have meant by it, the more I feel unsettled.

"Sure," I say, although I'm wondering if it's a good idea to keep spending time with him. I wonder if it's okay to keep going on dates with him knowing that he'll be leaving soon. Am I just setting myself up for a letdown here?

Part of me hopes Lukas will reach out for my hand, touch my hair, or….

I find myself gazing at his lips.

No. Cally's number one rule: never kiss a man when you're feeling unsure. I look away from the temptation.

Lukas takes a step forward. I can't tell what face he's making or where he's looking. I just see the nice pair of black loafers get closer.

"You look really nice today," I say, even though I don't know why. It's true though. He said we should dress up for Cascade since it's an upscale place, so I'm wearing a dress and heels. Meanwhile, he is back in his slacks and a white button-down. Even the casual clothes didn't last long. I want to laugh about that, but I don't.

"You, too," he says gently. Again, he sounds so sincere, but I suddenly don't want to hear it. "You look beautiful."

"Well," I mutter, still looking at the ground. "Thanks again. Goodbye."

I spin around and shut the door behind me, barely catching his voice as I go.

As I drag my feet into my bedroom, I catch sight of myself in the mirror. I look nice enough, a little fancier than usual, maybe like the type of woman Lukas would date. But did I feel like me? I kick off my heels and pull my hair out of its low bun.

Don't be dumb, I silently tell myself in the mirror. There's no use in thinking about dating someone who has every intention of leaving this place. It's only a matter of time.

I flop onto my bed and pull my body pillow into a tight squeeze. Tess uses the bench at the foot of the bed to hop up and lie in front of me. I stroke her fur and stare at the wall. I'm not sure how long I've been lying there, but my arm goes numb, and I'm feeling too lazy to move. Then I hear my door open and the familiar shuffle of Aunt Bev's footsteps wandering around my house. I know it's her because she's the only one with a key.

Knowing she'll find me, I stay silent and just focus on the sound of her socked feet patting the floor, getting closer and closer to my room. She comes through the opening and meets my eyes.

"Hi," I say, my voice slightly muffled by the pillow.

"Hi," she responds. She comes over to the bed and slides in beside me. I finally move, and Tess gets up with me as I sit up to wrap my arm around Aunt Bev.

"I couldn't do it," she whispers into my hair.

I know she's talking about today, Uncle Henry's birthday.

"I went to the baseball game, ordered a hotdog and a lite beer, but by the last half of the first inning I was crying," she says. Her voice sounds a little raw, so I guess she must have been crying for a while.

"I'm sorry I wasn't here," I say, lying my arm over hers and holding her hand.

She takes in a deep breath and lets out a jagged little exhale. "I need to do this by myself eventually," she tells herself more than me. "I can't depend on you forever."

"But I'll be here if you need me."

"I know."

We sit like that together for a while. Tess even falls asleep on my lap and lets out little whimpers in her sleep. Finally, my aunt breaks the silence.

"How was your date?" she asks.

I wiggle, unsure how to answer.

"Not good?" Aunt Bev asks.

I sigh. "It was great, actually, a little too great for someone who's bound to leave in less than a month."

Some of these moments with Lukas have been unexpected, blissful, magical even. There's no doubt that I'm interested in him, that I like him, even. But reality has hit me like a wrecking ball. If I really felt that magic, did it break already? Is it that fragile?

My aunt sits up and rests her hand on my side, patting it like my mom used to do to help me fall asleep when I was sick. "I'll tell you something," she says with a quiver in her voice. "You can't live life on what ifs, and you can't deny what's in front of you, even if it's bound to leave you. Autumn–" She takes a breath. "Love is magic, no matter how long it lasts. Maybe it's a flash. Maybe it's a whole slow motion silent film. But you can't really measure it."

I feel a little silly. Aunt Bev is having a heart-wrenching day mourning another missed birthday of her lost husband while I'm sulking over a potentially failing but very new courtship. I look up at her, expecting to find her with tears in her eyes, but she seems a little stronger somehow, and that in itself makes me want to cry.

"I thought it could be magic, but I think the spell's breaking before it's really even started," I admit.

She gives me a tender smile and traces my cheek with her warm hand. "I think the magic is very much alive," she says. "Sometimes you just lose sight of it. It's all part of the appeal."

I smile wryly.

"So what's wrong, exactly?" she asks. "He's in town for a short time, and you can't see him just because of that?"

It's hard to answer her when she puts it that way.

"Have you ever regretted a trip with your parents, even though you knew it would end and that you'd come back home after the couple of weeks were up?" she asks.

I think about it and shake my head.

"Have you enjoyed your time with him so far?"

I'd be lying if I suggested anything other than yes. I nod.

"Then maybe you can think of it in that line. Just keep seeing him and see where it goes. Take a metaphorical trip with him. Make some memories, share some experiences." My aunt changes position, her legs crossed. The life in her eyes and skin has returned.

I readjust myself, too, careful not to rustle the sleeping pup too much, and face her. I spot a few more gray hairs that I hadn't noticed before. "I'm not sure," I admit. "Wouldn't that just make it harder to say goodbye?"

She shimmies a shrug. "Why think about the end when you're only at the beginning?"

I want to ask her if she's always been this paradoxical, this mysteriously wise.

But before I get a chance, she gets up and pulls me along with her. "Enough moping. We're making cinnamon rolls."

THE NEXT AFTERNOON AT WORK ON THE TOUR BUS, GUS NOTICES immediately that I'm a little off.

"You're not sick, are you?" he asks, pushing a warm cup of tea into my hands. "There's peppermint in there. It'll soothe your stomach and throat."

I smile at him and thank him but assure him that I'm not sick.

He studies my face for a moment and then seems to realize something. "Then here," he says, pulling out a foil-wrapped heart-shaped chocolate from his jacket pocket. "For the love kind of sick."

Before I can correct him, he climbs into the bus and starts checking it over.

I'm not lovesick, I think, unwrapping the chocolate and breaking it in half. I pop the chocolate into my mouth. It's sweet and warm, but hard to swallow. I wrap up the other half for later and wash it down with the tea. It's a strange mix, but my nerves ease… a little.

I take a deep breath and prepare for the next group of tourists. I try to put on my usual excited persona. I want to give my customers a good experience. But it's not easy when you realize that the magic of love isn't all that it's cracked up to be when you realize it has no place in reality.

Maybe I've been dreaming with a false sense of the world for too long.

CHAPTER 14

It's strange. I wake up in the morning feeling lighter than a cloud, and not even a rain cloud–a white, fluffy, sunny day cloud. My first thought is of Autumn. I grab my phone and check it, not for emails from the Menendez Group, but for texts from her.

To my dismay, there's nothing since the messages sorting out our plans for the day before. But actually, I don't feel dismayed at all. It's early, only 6:30, so she probably isn't even awake yet. I jump out of bed, tug on a pair of shorts and one of my T-shirts, and jog downstairs to the exercise parlor. I'm not surprised when I'm the only one there. After a couple of hours of weight training, I check my phone again. Still nothing. I text her a quick, "Good morning," slide it back in my pocket, and take a shower.

I check my phone after breakfast. Nothing.

I check it after lunch. Nothing.

Then I check it a few more times before 9:00 P.M. Still nothing.

I'm feeling dismayed for real this time. I type out a text to check in. When I wake up the next morning... zilch.

My stomach sinks. Our date was good… great. Both of them were. She had been a bit quiet on the drive back from our meal in Grant, but I thought she was just preoccupied with her aunt. I replay our conversations from that day. I remember telling her I think she's beautiful and telling her that I've really enjoyed spending time with her so far.

Where did I go wrong? It's a thought that continues to haunt me.

Days later, Julia is still lurking around me and irking me more than ever. But right now after not hearing a word from Autumn for a few days, she's the only one I can talk to. Thomas, Miles, and Braden went on some kind of a hike that I didn't feel like taking, so I declined. Now it's just me and Julia in the common room, with her seated a little too close to me.

"Have you ever been ghosted?" I ask her out of the blue.

She scoffs. "Yeah, by you."

I frown. "I mean, by a guy you like."

Julia is quiet, her expression thoughtful, which is rare. "Is there… someone you like?" she finally asks.

I don't feel like putting my whole heart out on my sleeve, not for her. But this whole thing with Autumn is new. And hopefully these last few days are just a fluke and our… whatever it is… is not already doomed. "I've just… texted someone several times over the last three days and haven't heard anything back yet."

Julia looks at me with a faint crease between her two eyebrows, and she's chewing on the inside of her cheek. "I don't know," she says. It's curt, a little harsh. And it catches me off guard.

Why am I talking to her about this?

"Where is everyone?" I ask, looking around. "I haven't seen anybody but you today."

"I dunno."

I glance down at my watch. I think the pottery class is soon, so I rise abruptly.

"Where are you going?" Julia grabs my sweater sleeve.

"To a class next door." As much as it surprised me, I had a lot of fun with the first class. I think it'd be fun to try it again. Plus, I need something to get my mind off Autumn. It's making the days so long.

Julia goes back to looking annoyed. I pull my arm from her grasp and head next door to the event building. But the other couple of guys in our group are standing on the porch talking about work.

"The Fin-vice pres wants to acquire another company, to merge with a similar sized financial management company in the Upper East Side. Something about accessing new clientele," Carlos says.

This piques my interest, and I forget about the class, crossing my arms and joining in on the conversation. Once I help the Menendez group get on their feet, I'll have the space to take on another client.

A short time later, the three hikers come back, and we head back to the common area.

"You all are back soon," I tell them.

Miles pats Branden on the shoulder. "This old man is a little out of shape. Don't make him feel bad about it."

Branden shakes his head and mutters, "I'm only thirty-five."

"Besides," Thomas chimes in, "while we were out, we got to talking about this new acquisition. Any kind of merger comes with a new mishmash of change."

"Mishmash?" Julia mocks, stepping up behind us.

With that, we're off to the races. This is where I shine, making plans to make the most out of the situation so I can get ahead in the company. Doing this kind of thing scratches that hard-to-reach itch on my brain.

I let myself get sucked in and do as Branden intended–bond with the team. We talk about our strong suits, our successes, the areas we aren't confident in. We share ideas about business models and goals and seven-step plans. An hour bleeds into four, and before I know it it's lunchtime.

I freshen up in my room and stretch out my stiff body. I feel worn out, probably because my brain has been on vacation for too long. "You lose the muscles you don't use," my old high school football coach used to tell us. It's probably true in the business world as well.

Man, I haven't thought of high school in so long. I used to think my dad was mad at me for not trying to play football in college, but he adamantly denied any ill feelings about my life choices.

It's midday, and the dull slate gray sky is growing brighter as the clouds disperse. Out of nowhere, I miss my parents. I can't remember the last time I talked to them. I always spend so much time at work that they slip my mind or it's too late to call.

A gaggle of geese flies over the pond in a V formation. I watch them circle around and then skid and splash mostly gracefully into the glittering water. My chest feels tight, heavy, hot.

I pull out my phone and bring up my dad's number. It looks foreign to me, and a shot of guilt strikes me in the throat. I should know this number by heart, but I don't.

I call him, and the phone rings and rings but goes to voicemail. I don't know what to say anyway, so I hang up without leaving a message.

In the reflection of the bay window, I'm reminded of Autumn. I'm wearing the white cable-knit sweater again that I bought on our date. It's actually very comfortable, and I do like the way it looks, even if it looks like I'm trying to be something—someone—I never imagined myself to be.

My phone vibrates in my hand. I think it might be my father calling, but it's a text from Autumn. It just says, "Hi," and I answer her immediately.

My chest twists in a new way, remembering how at ease I felt with her. Even when we discussed hard topics, I didn't avoid them. I gaze out the window, wondering how Autumn would see this scene. She'd probably giggle at the way the geese's heads disappear when they curl up to sleep. She'd probably know where they came from, where they're going, and the names of their flight patterns. She'd tell me all of that, and I'd eat it up because she was just so good at making everything interesting.

During lunch, everyone is buzzing with anticipation from the earlier company talk. They're typing emails and trying to take phone calls with clients. And I'm doing the same. I haven't spoken with anyone from the Menendez Group for at least two days, so I make sure to catch up with them and update them on step three of our seven-step plan.

Branden steals our attention with a couple of loud claps. "Hey, Team! You might have noticed that we're all in the same place, and you know what that means," he leads us on cheerily. "Team-building exercises!"

At least one person groans, though I'm not sure who.

"Don't worry," Branden shouts. "This will be fun. We're going to play some games!"

Christopher looks up from his phone for the first time. "What kind of games, exactly? Will it be long? I was just getting back in touch with Saffire Enterprises again… I was going to call them."

"Nope!" Branden says. "Reschedule! Consider the whole rest of the day blocked off."

Miles's shoulders slump a little, and Thomas looks over at me. I shrug. Whatever is about to happen wasn't on our original itinerary.

"You have twenty minutes to get dressed into the most comfortable, sport-friendly thing you brought!"

"Sport-friendly?" I mutter aloud. What could that mean?

I take this free moment to check my messages. There are a few emails, but I click on the text from Autumn. She asks what I'm doing today. I tell her about the mystery team-building exercises and that I'm not sure what to expect. I slide my phone back in my pocket, feeling a little revived just from that short exchange.

As instructed, all Fin-vice team members met on the front porch. Thomas was wearing the sweats I'd seen him in a couple of times, and a few of the guys were even in their slacks, but Julia was wearing what appeared to be silk pajama bottoms and a borrowed Fin-vice T-shirt from Branden that he had worn the other day.

"Don't look at me like that," Julia says with her arms crossed. "Nobody said anything about sports!"

Ivy meets us on the porch and tells us what's in store, noting the volleyball net set up in the front yard and a mystery box that she's holding.

First task: a simple hike up around the lake. This, I'm sure, is just

Branden's way of warming everyone up for task two. Second task: a friendly game of volleyball in which more than half of the team is uncomfortable. We split up into a team of three and a team of four. I'm grateful that Julia is on my side for once because when Miles hits a ball and almost nails her in the side of the head, she nearly freezes him with her icy death stare. It's all a little bit fun though, and it feels good to move around. Third task: a thrilling round of company trivia. It's safe to say nobody but Branden is excited for this one. We might all be dedicated workers, but I doubt any of us are on that level. It turns out that our answers are clues for task four: a scavenger hunt.

We've spent almost three whole hours as a group. Everyone checks their phones for emails every chance they get, and by luck of the draw, I'm paired with Julia for the scavenger hunt. She leans against me and hangs on my arm as we walk around looking for our next item on the checklist, something edible that grows out of the ground. I try to stay focused on the task, even though I'm getting worn out and I want to see if I have any messages from the Menendez group… or Autumn. Still, it's tough to ignore Julia's constant presence and her incessant huffing and whining.

By some miracle, we finish our checklist in an hour, and by then, the sun is starting to dull. Branden asks if we had fun, and I try to give him an encouraging smile, but my mind keeps drifting off and I can't commit to it.

"Lukey?" Julia whispers.

I look down at her. Her hair's a little frizzy , and her mascara is slightly smudged. I wonder how loud she'll shriek when she sees herself in the next reflective surface. I want to stand her in front of the window so I can see the scene now.

"Let's eat dinner together," she suggests.

"I think everyone's—"

"No," she interrupts. She gnaws on the inside of her cheek. "I mean just you and me. I found an interesting place in town."

I'm not thrilled about spending another hour with her, but I have to admit that it would be nice to get out of the inn for the evening. I've just been wandering from porch to exercise parlor to my room to the kitchen for the last couple of days. According to Autumn's last text, she's helping Cally make some Halloween costumes. Maybe I could swing by her place after we eat....

"I guess that's fine," I say slowly. "But don't you hate this dinky little town? Are you sure you want to go back into it and mingle there?"

She twists her shoulders. "I need a change of scenery. I want to find someplace nice."

"Nice...?"

She nods. "Don't worry. It's just food, not a date or anything."

CHAPTER 15

THREE DAYS WITHOUT LUKAS HAS BEEN HARD. I'VE PICKED UP MY PHONE so many times between tours and during breaks, wanting to text him back but feeling unsure what to say. I'm still torn between taking my aunt's advice and protecting my heart. It stung when he said he was excited to go back to New York. And I know that when he said he had enjoyed his time with me, he meant it... but it also made me question his intentions. Frankly, I'm too scared to find out.

Today, I have a full day off with no obligations to Blue Kiss or to Maple Falls Touring. I sleep in and then take Tess to the dog park and for a little jog around the block. Work has been helping—a little—but now my thoughts keep landing on Lukas. Every time I turn a corner, I think of what I might do if he happens to be standing there. And when I arrive home from my jog with Tess, I secretly hope he's waiting out back again.

But he isn't. I wonder what he's doing now. Should I text him?

My phone buzzes, and my heart leaps at the thought of who it could be. But when I pull it out, it's Cally.

You're still coming by to help today, right?

It takes a second for me to realize what she's talking about. Crap. I forgot that I had promised Cally and her little cousins during her birthday party that I'd help them sew their Halloween costumes today. Halloween is coming soon, and most kids want to wear their costumes during the festival, which is even sooner.

I stare down at my phone. Lukas is going to have to wait a little longer.

I type out a text to Cally. *Yeah. I'll come by in 30.*

I'm about to round up Tess and my sewing supplies, but first, I open up a different conversation and send a simple text. Hi.

It feels like I'm in high school again, texting a boy I have a crush on. Well... I suppose that's still the case now, except I'm ten years older with more complicated thoughts and emotions. I switch my phone to silent mode so I don't feel tempted to answer him too soon.

When I arrive at Cally's house, the kids are stuffing their faces with chocolate pudding at the kitchen table. Jack is spooning in heaps with one hand while reading an illustrated Charlie Brown book with the other. Meena is standing at the head wearing a pair of ballet flats and practicing third position. She kicks out a leg when she sees me and gives a big, chocolatey smile. Jihwan is sitting on the table criss-cross with a spoon in each hand.

"You're here!" Cally cheers. "I had to bribe them with pudding to get them to stay in one spot while I took their measurements."

"I did a good job, though," Meena says.

Cally chuckles. "Of course. The model student. She held a perfect second position the whole time."

Meena gives a self-assured smile and takes another bite of chocolate pudding.

It sounds like we have a lot to do after Cally shows me the plans for each costume. "What happened to the banana character for Meena?" I ask.

"Something about wanting to fit in better with the other girls, I think," she says with a hint of sadness.

I don't remember being that age and thinking those kinds of

things, but I do remember that middle school in general was a tough time. It's hard to find your place sometimes. But it makes my heart droop knowing that Meena was looking forward to being that Hanana character and chose to go with a standard princess like so many other girls.

"At least it'll be easier to make, I guess," Cally says after a moment.

"But, uh… what about this? Is it a squid?" I ask, picking up a long purple tentacle of some kind.

Cally laughs. "Jihwan wants to be a purple octopus. My mom showed me how to make that tentacle, but we've got six and a half more to do…."

Oh, boy.

For the next couple of hours, we let the kids help us take part in making their costumes. Jack's is the simplest, as we only need to make his navy blue striped shirt and a hat and add a couple of patches to a pair of already exciting overalls. Meena is a good helper, but she works slowly so that every cut is as perfect as possible. And she keeps wanting to add a fuller skirt and more layers of the glittery fabric. I'm getting a little worried that she'll end up looking like an eighties fairy godmother, but it's still fun. Jihwan's purple octopus costume, on the other hand, is quite the handful. Actually, it's eight handfuls. And after two hours, Cally has finished only two legs.

"That's an hour a leg!" she bemoans. But I can tell that she's actually having fun. The kids seem to be, too.

Jihwan tugs on my pants leg. "I'm hungry," he says. His eyes are so big and brown, he looks like a precious little doll. My heart melts at the innocent way he holds onto my leg and looks up at me.

"I guess it's break time then! Who wants grilled cheese?" I ask.

Jack literally jumps out of his chair. "Grilled cheese?!"

I'm surprised at his sudden excitement. He's usually so reserved.

"Guess we know your favorite meal, then." Cally laughs.

We take a break and make grilled cheese sandwiches. After getting the kids settled at the table, I check my phone. I force myself to contain a smile when I see I have a message waiting from Lukas. It just says, "Good Morning," but there's a cheery-looking emoji attached. I look at the time. He must have answered as soon as he got my first text because it was delivered one minute after my message.

"What's that look?" Cally asks, nudging my shoulder.

I quickly hide my phone in my back pocket and take up a plate of grilled cheese. Cally keeps looking at me through narrowed eyes, but she doesn't pry. When she leaves the table to refill Jack's cup of milk, I send another text to ask what Lukas is doing today.

Three hours later, when we've added the last puffy sleeve and last glittery layer, the kids are getting restless. They wiggle and squirm as we make sure their costumes are fitted right. They look pretty good except for a few places that need to be taken in on the fairy princess dress. And we opted for only making six octopus legs, thinking it wouldn't hurt for two of Jihwan's human legs to count for two of the eight. He doesn't seem to mind, and he loves spinning and jumping around threatening to ink us.

We all play in the backyard and make a little obstacle course out of twigs and blankets and ending in a pile of raked up leaves. We're having a great time when the kids' parents come to pick them up. I say hello to Cally's older sister and her older brother and his wife and say goodbye to the kids. They're raving about their costumes and talking about the obstacle course. I, for one, and feeling a little exhausted, and that grilled cheese didn't tide me over for long.

My stomach growls, prompting Cally to ask if I want to go get some dinner. I nod, and while she's freshening up in the bathroom, I check my phone. There's nothing from Lukas since his earlier message explaining he was about to partake in some mysterious team activities. I decide to let him be and don't send another message. He needs to focus on whatever those activities are.

I take my turn to freshen up and borrow a sweat-free, dirt-stain-free sweater from Cally. Since she lives in the middle of town, we opt to walk to the closest restaurant a few blocks away, The Snapdragon. It's a cute little joint with a sleek modern vibe. It's one of the more somewhat upscale places in town, the kind where kids will go for dinner on prom night or couples will go to celebrate their anniversaries. I don't go often, and when I step inside, it reminds me a bit of a smaller, simpler version of Cascade, where Lukas last took me.

"What're you thinking about?" Cally asks as we sit down. "You're a little quieter than usual."

I offer a tight smile. "I'm just thinking about Lukas," I admit. "I mean, I feel kind of bad for not messaging him much these last couple of days. We were having such a good time together, and then I started overthinking it and freaked myself out."

Cally rests her cheek in her hand and stares at me like the loving friend she is. "I kind of agree with your aunt on this one," she says. "I think it's better for you to do what makes you happy, and I can tell you that you've been different these last few days. Before you psyched yourself out and you were enjoying your time with him, you were so… bright." She made a big bursting gesture. "Like something magical," she adds.

I roll my eyes. Not that word again. I don't think I'm ready for magic after all.

"Really!" she says with a giant smile. "You reminded me of your aunt, you know, back then."

Thankfully, a waiter comes and takes our drink order so I don't have to respond to her and tell her I had thought the same thing for a moment. It's too scary to say aloud, to admit that kind of grand thing after such a short time. Plus, one fact hasn't changed. He's going to leave.

Cally and I resume our conversation about the upcoming Autumn Leaves Celebration, but the door chimes, and a familiar tall, charcoal-suited man steps through the door. I almost call out to him, but then another familiar blonde businesswoman comes in behind him. They get seated across the room from us in a cozy booth next to the window. I watch the whole time, wondering if anyone else from their team was going to join them.

Then a pair of icy blue eyes captures mine. Julia looks at me, and in less than a few seconds, three different looks cross her face: indifference, then surprise… then… cunning? She leans across the table and places her hand on Lukas's arm. I can only see the back of his head, but I don't need to see anything else after she gets out of her side of the booth and sidles up next to him.

"I need to go," I mutter.

Cally cocks her head at me.

"I want to go," I say through my teeth, grabbing my purse.

My friend looks around the room and then spots the reason for my sudden change in attitude. I take off, leaving her to pay for our barely touched colas, and I fight the stinging in my throat and eyes as I swiftly move out the door.

"What the heck?" I hear Cally growl behind me a second later. "Is he—"

"I think I misunderstood his character," I say. I clutch my embroidered black cat bag. "I just got my hopes up because I've been feeling lonely for a while, so I must have missed something. But I can't... date someone like that."

Without looking back to see if Lukas saw me or if that woman is still watching me, I pass their window and turn sharply down the street with Cally struggling to keep up.

CHAPTER 16

Tʜᴇ ʜᴏᴘᴇ ᴛʜᴀᴛ ʜᴀᴅ sᴡᴇʟʟᴇᴅ ɪɴ ᴍʏ ᴄʜᴇsᴛ ᴛʜᴀᴛ ɴɪɢʜᴛ Aᴜᴛᴜᴍɴ texted me back has been stomped down over the last week. We had two incredible dates that made me feel like a changed man, or at least a man who was willing to change, to get out of his pristine, perfectly planned life and try something out of his comfort zone, something that made him feel free. And now what? I have sent her text after text and heard nothing. The only reason I know she's still alive is because I asked Ivy. I correctly assumed they were friends. I'd seen them talk on our first day here, and Autumn had mentioned her in a couple of stories about her life here in Maple Falls.

Needless to say, I'm confused. I'm confused by Autumn and confused by myself. I came to know her as an easy-going, free-spirited woman who could make anything interesting, as a smart hard-worker who never asked for extravagant things. She helped me to relax and see the beauty of the world around me. She helped me to breathe and think about what might make me feel fulfilled. She made me want to ask myself hard questions and get the answers.

And now Autumn has been stripped away from my life. She had lifted me up so high, and now I feel like I'm left hanging like the last overripe pear.

I shake my head like a wet Labrador as I step out of the shower, flinging off thoughts of Autumn away along with the droplets of water.

Without Autumn, the last week has been just me filling my time in whatever way I can. I haven't stayed at the inn during the day anymore. I'm too restless there, so I have been visiting the town. One day I even stumbled upon a group of people playing volleyball in the park. They caught me watching and asked if I wanted to play. I almost said no, but thought better. What do I have to lose? Over the week, I had tried a couple of other restaurants and visited the little Maple Falls town museum. It was interesting, but I found myself wishing that Autumn was there to speak the words to me rather than having to read the town's story from a pamphlet. I even attended church for the first time since I left home.

But the main reason I've been spending more time away from the inn is because it's uncomfortable there with Julia hovering over me all the time. Ever since that night I went to dinner with her, she's been completely in my space. She said it herself—it wasn't a date—so why is she now acting like I belong to her? I keep thinking I need to have a talk with her, but I don't know how to begin. I think I'm starting to see what's got her acting this way, and it's been going on for far too long. I need to put a stop to it soon.

For a split second, I consider sending another text to Autumn, but I don't want to seem pushy. It's been a full week since I heard from her, and now I'll be leaving in just a couple of days. Maybe it's time to let her go.

The thought makes me feel strange. God knows I don't want to say goodbye to her, but what can I do if she won't even give me the time of day?

Throwing my phone on the bed, I get dressed in the jeans and boots I bought with Autumn before our first date. They're feeling more and more comfortable as I wear them, and I can't imagine how I ever got used to slacks. I shuffle through the sweaters I bought that day and settle on a green one. I picked it because it reminded me of her eyes.

What a lovesick fool, I chide myself.

I pull the sweater over my head and go outside. The air has grown chillier and a bit more dry. So many more of the leaves have darkened from their yellows and golds into orange and red. Many more have fallen onto the ground, too, and the older dried ones crunch under my feet as I walk down to the lake and observe the geese for a while.

Later, I decide to partake in my third pottery class. I force myself to focus on the way the cool clay feels in my hands as I shape it, finding the perfect level of pressure to make the desired shape. I can't say that it looks perfect, but I'm satisfied when I form an oblong bowl. The instructor offers to fire it for me, and I'm actually excited to see how it'll turn out. I ask if it will be ready by the time I left in a couple of days, and she says that she'll try her best.

Thomas catches me on my way across the yard. "Hey, man, I haven't seen you around much. What's going on? We're going to have an impromptu meeting to discuss the merger again." He claps me on the shoulder and gives it a squeeze. "That's a rad sweater."

I grimace at him. "People don't say rad anymore."

He mocks me. "Okay, Julia. Geez, you've been spending too much time together. You're starting to make the same face she makes."

I shake off his hand. "No, we haven't, and no, I'm not. I haven't even talked to her aside from the stupid team meetings." I feel angry, unsettled. I can't explain it, but it makes me feel jittery. I just want to feel at ease again like I did with....

"Sorry, dude. I was just kidding, though that does explain why she's been especially sour the last few days," he says. "Anyway, where'd you get that sweater? I like it."

"Autumn," I say. Her name feels like honey on my tongue, a little weighty and sweet.

"You, uh... gonna see her again?" he asks.

I sigh. "I'm not sure what happened, but I haven't heard from her."

My buddy lets out a knowing, ahh. "Well, you know where to find her, right?"

All I can do is stare blankly.

He shakes his head. "You trying to tell me Mister Planner Man didn't think of that?"

I scoff. "Of course I thought about seeing her but… I didn't think… about going to her."

Thomas smacks me on the back, jarring me. "Then go see her, you big oaf."

I'm standing in front of the inn waiting for the tour bus to pull in. My hands are shaking more than I'd like to admit. And I don't even want to know what my hair looks like with the amount of times I've raked my hands through it. Thanks to the tour's website, I was able to book an individual tour where I can get on the bus from my location and ride with the group along the route.

Finally, when the bus pulls up, my heart is in my throat. Autumn steps out and the wind catches her hair, blowing it across her beautiful face. She swipes her hair out of her eyes and sees me. First she looks surprised, then her demeanor turns… angry. I clench my teeth. Just what has her feeling this way about me? I thought I made it clear that I liked her.

I walk over to her, but she won't look straight at me. Her cheeks are a bit red, but I don't think it's from a shy blush this time.

"Autumn?" I say her name, but she doesn't look up. Gulping down the hard rock that is my heart, I realize just how hard it's going to be to say goodbye to her. And even if she's mad at me now, I don't want to leave her this way. Maybe… maybe that's what this is. Could she be mad that I'm leaving?

Thinking back to our conversation, which I'd replayed hundreds of times by now, her behavior changed just after I told her I was excited to go back home.

My heart squeezes, and I want to reach out and hug her close to me. But I restrain myself—for now. "It's good to see you," I tell her before I climb onto the bus.

When the tour starts back up, Autumn is trying hard not to look at me, but I see her gazing out of the corner of her eye as she gestures to the outside world we're passing through. We stop at the blue bridge, The Kissing Bridge, and everyone gets off the bus.

I find her, even though she's trying to keep her back to me. "Autumn," I say, touching her hand.

She curls it up and walks away, striking up a conversation with a couple of other passengers about the name of the color of the bridge: cerulean. As we get back on the bus, I try again, but she shakes her head at me. Funny how a shake of the head can make me feel the slightest bit of hope. At least she acknowledged me.

I try to talk to her again at the orchard, then again at a cave that we didn't stop at before. I track along behind her as she guides us, never tearing my gaze away. How could she be so stoic? Where did her bright liveliness go? Was this all really because of me leaving? How can I find out if she won't talk to me?

When the bus tour is nearing its conclusion, I decide to stop trying. I don't even get off the bus at the last stop before my final opportunity. Instead, I wrestle with my thoughts. Is it better to just let her be mad? She clearly isn't going to speak to me, for whatever reason. As much as it hurts, I think I just have to tell her goodbye and not expect anything else from her. Maybe I can still thank her for the new sense of self she'd helped me find, even if it was one-sided.

The bus brakes shriek as it stops in front of the inn. Autumn leads the way off, and a couple of others get off before me. On my way out, I thank the old man driving and stop next to Autumn for the last time.

"Autumn," I say, reluctant to say the words but knowing I have no choice. "Please, just let me say goodbye to you. I–"

"Goodbye," she repeats coldly, cutting me off.

I'm actually stunned. It feels like I've been stabbed in the stomach. This... this isn't right. It's not supposed to be like this.

Autumn gets back on the bus, and the doors cut through the cavernous space between us.

CHAPTER 17

SEEING LUKAS YESTERDAY ONLY MADE ME FEEL MORE SICK. I FEEL awful for ignoring him and saying such an angry goodbye, but I'm hurt! No matter how good a time we had and how much I feel–felt—I liked him, I don't deserve to get strung along like that.

It's one thing to tell me that he's excited to go back to New York, which I know is where his life is. Even if he's not happy with it, that's his decision. Even though I can see how Maple Falls has loosened him up and brought him down to earth, he is the one who gets to make his decisions for his life.

It's another thing to leave me after making me feel hope for magic and love and all that nonsense, but it's another to straight up lie to me! He said that he wasn't involved with Julia, and I believed him. I let him make me feel like I was the only girl in the world for him, but he had her in his back pocket the whole time.

So yeah. I'm angry. I didn't want to say goodbye, but he insisted, so I said it. That was more than he deserved.

Yet... my insides are all knotted up like a creepy twisted tree in a

Halloween movie. I can't sleep at night, and it's giving me dark circles under my eyes. I can't even make myself enjoy this day–my favorite out of the whole year! We're getting ready for the Autumn Leaves Celebration, but I'm so preoccupied thinking about Lukas planting himself hundreds of miles away from me.

Yes, this is better. It's better than getting even more attached and letting him take my whole heart with him. At least... at least I managed to keep it. Most of it.

"Ugh, I just can't believe I was so off base with him!" I tell Aunt Bev. "And, like, how is it possible that I'm still thinking about him and feeling sad that he's leaving even after I saw them together? What is wrong with me?"

My lovely aunt puts her hands on mine, which have been roughly moving baked goods from the box to the table, and looks me in the face. She sucks in a purposeful breath, silently encouraging me to do the same. I comply, and together, we breathe in deeply and out slowly.

"Now," she says, wrapping her cool fingers around mine. "Don't beat yourself up for falling in love. It happens to the best of us."

"Hah!" I laugh a little bit too loudly. Someone across the street throws back a worried look at us. "Love! As if! We only went on two dates!"

Aunt Bev gives me a lopsided smile. "And sometimes it only takes one look."

I gnash my teeth together and shake my head. "No. It's not love. That's ridiculous."

"Autumn," she says calmly. "I'm not here trying to convince you that you were or are in love with Lukas, but it seems like you're spending an awful lot of energy trying to convince yourself you're not."

Hot tears sting my eyes, but I will them to stop. "I just... I thought we...." I don't even know what to say, so I stop there.

"Listen, honey," she says, wiping away a warm tear that got away. "What's important is that you're honest with yourself. Fighting what happened or what could happen only takes you out of the moment. I know it hurts to think someone you thought highly of could be flawed in such a way, but you're only being discourteous to yourself and to the good parts of them that that person showed you."

I choke down the lump rising in my throat. I know that Lukas showed me some genuine parts of himself. It just turns out that there are other parts of him that I didn't expect. I take in another deep breath.

"You know, Henry wasn't perfect either," Aunt Bev says, getting a far-off look in her eyes. "He never hid another woman from me, I know, but he did hide a sickness. And for a while, I hated him because of that. I tortured myself with that hate and ended up wasting some precious time."

"I don't understand. Are you saying I should—"

"I'm not saying you should forgive him for seeing that other woman," she says. "Of course not. I'm just saying that you can't let that anger distract you from what's in front of you now. This is your favorite time of year, and I've never seen you so glum and gloomy." She dusted off the invisible worries from my shoulders.

I nodded. "Okay."

EVERY FALL AT THE FESTIVAL GROUNDS, PEOPLE SPEND TWO DAYS setting up different booths and activities. The whole town comes together to create a magical realm of fall and Halloween, the perfect mix between cozy and spooky. For many years I've helped the decorating committee, so it's my job to make sure we succeed in getting that perfect mix. Cally and Ivy are both part of the planning committee, and they're in charge of the activities and amusement. Cally is working on some kind of giant hay maze, and Ivy is working on securing a tractor and route for the hayride.

Everyone is putting in a lot of work to make this night fun for the town, so I don't have time to cry about my whiplash feelings for Lukas or my disappointment. I need to focus on my job today so we can have a successful festival tomorrow.

Tonight's biggest goal is to put the finishing touches on the haunted house. Normally I would make friendly conversation with the characters, many of whom are current seniors in high school, and get their opinion on the set-up. This year, though, I mostly keep my head down and keep to myself.

I'm trying to be my normal self, but I just feel off. My mind keeps circling with thoughts of Lukas like a desperate vulture. A stupid, desperate vulture. How can he affect me so much? It's just not fair. Meanwhile, he seems to be fine... at least, aside from the dozens of texts he sent that I left unanswered.

I want to forget about him and block his number, but every time I get a text, it sparks a tiny flame of hope. I just can't do it. Not yet. I need to wallow in it a little bit more first.

Soon Cally finds them with a sweet delivery: a warm cinnamon cider and a toasty apple turnover from her mother's baked goods table. The cinnamon cider feels good in my hands, which have become a little cool from the night air. It's already getting chilly at night, which means that Halloween will probably be cold this year. I wonder if we should add a lining to better insulate Cally's cousins' costumes....

"Take a bite," Cally demands.

I look up at her from the cinderblock I'm sitting on. I obey and bite off a small corner of the turnover. It's perfectly crispy, and the cinnamony goodness inside takes nice and sweet. But my stomach churns, and I don't think I can take another bite.

"I'm sorry," I say when she sees me lower the rest of the turnover. "It's really tasty. I'm just not hungry right now."

Cally crosses her arms. I can tell she's upset with me. Probably annoyed. But instead of scolding me, she just nods her head and says, "This is the worst fall yet."

I obviously have to agree.

"You've still got a long way to go," she continues, not even looking at me. "But it'll get better. It just feels like a lot because it's fresh. You'll feel better about things soon. You'll be able to move on be ready to fall again for a guy who's better for you, for a guy who doesn't see other woman and who will chase after you and make sure you have everything you could desire."

My heart twists, and a sneaky tear streams down my cheek. "This is so silly," I say, wiping it away a slightly angrily. "I can't believe I… that he…."

Cally squats down next to me and pats me on the knee. "I know, Autumn."

"I was scared to like him so much when I know he's leaving," I continue. "But as soon as I felt like taking the chance anyway, I saw them together. Now I just feel like a fool."

"You're not a fool," Cally coos. "You're just a girl who fell for a guy. That happens sometimes. All the time, actually."

I shake my head. "I should have been more careful or something. But I thought I felt it."

Cally studies my face for a moment before asking, "Felt what, exactly?"

I twist the corner of the napkin that's wrapped around the apple turnover. "I dunno. Magic, I guess."

This is the first time I think that Cally looks at me with pity. It's similar to the look she gives my aunt sometimes, like she's so sad to see her hurting but she doesn't know how to make it better. We're both sitting in silence with townspeople and strangers alike passing us on both sides. My heart is cracked, but the world is carrying on. It's not like I expected it to stop for me or anything, but at the same time, I don't want time to take me away from those good feelings I shared with Lukas. Even if they ended this way, even if I might resent him for hurting me….

"It's just that it felt so nice to be seen," I say. I'm slightly surprised by the shake in my voice. "To have someone look at me like that. It was exciting every time he showed me another part of himself. I guess I just got too greedy."

Cally shakes her head. "I've never been in love before, at least not the real kind," she tells me. "And maybe I don't understand it or know how it's supposed to feel. But, hun, I think you'll know when it's real. It'll really feel like magic. It'll be unexplainable and undeniable. And maybe it won't happen at first sight. Maybe it'll take a year or more. But when it comes, I'm sure some of this pain will melt away. So just don't give up, okay?"

My best friend is always supportive. She's always my rock and my neon arrow. We don't always see eye-to-eye, but she always makes sure to help me stay true to myself. And I love her so much for that.

"You're too good to me," I tell her with a pitiful laugh.

She smiles and stands, offering her hand.

"I'm not giving up," I tell her. "Maybe there's some sort of magical, unexplainable love waiting for me. But right now, it just sucks a little."

She takes the apple turnover from my hand and puts it to my mouth. I take another bite and find that it's still warm, still sweet. My stomach doesn't deny it, so I eat a couple more bites.

"Maybe I'm just looking for the wrong kind of magic," I say as we stroll through the crowd of busy festival workers. "Maybe I should try falling in love with summer or something," I say with a wry laugh.

CHAPTER 18

"Are you stalling?" Thomas asks, sticking his head into my room. It's the third time he's been by, but I'm surprised when his head pops around the door.

He stares at me while I sit on the corner of the bed with my elbows on my knees and my suitcase splayed open. I've been "packing" for over an hour, and it seems like every time I put something in my suitcase, my body gets heavier.

"Why would I be stalling?" I ask myself more than him. It's not a rhetorical question.

Thomas steps inside the room and pushes the door closed behind him. "You've been weird for the last couple of days. I mean, you've been different since the first week, more relaxed... less attached to work stuff, but now it's a weird kind of different."

I don't know what to say, so I just stay silent and fall back onto the mattress.

"Lukas, really," he says, sounding genuinely concerned. "What's going on?"

I cover my face with my hands and block out the light. "My chest feels all tight. My mind is always racing. I don't have any desire to work. And I just want... to see her. I don't want her to be angry with me. Whatever I did, I want to make it right."

The other corner of the bed shifts with Thomas's weight. "Wow, I think this is the first time I've seen someone who is lovesick."

I peek around my palm and glare at him. "Don't mock me."

Thomas laughs. "I'm not mocking you! I mean it. This is wild. Like, what do I even do to help my best friend out?"

I pinch the bridge of my nose and will myself to sit up, though I stop on my elbow, half-reclined. "My body just feels so heavy," I explain. "That's the only way to say it. I don't know...."

Thomas steeples his hands and looks over at me seriously. "So your answer is to just... lay on this bed forever? Because the woman you like doesn't like you back?"

"She does, though!" I practically yell, surprising myself. I add with a more controlled tone, "I know she does."

Pressing his lips in a tight line, Thomas sharpens his gaze. "What do you want to do then?" What did you hope would come of this?"

"I don't know, man," I groan. "All I can say is that the couple of days that I spent with Autumn were the best days I've had in the last fifteen years of my life. I just wanted... to see where things went. I wanted to spend more time with her. She helped me relax and see the goodness in little things. I've been so wound up with work, I just want... to take a break from it all. I want to live my life outside of my office."

Thomas's eyebrows flinch up. "You're saying you'd rather be here than work?"

I shrug. "Yeah, maybe. I guess so. It's just... going back and facing those long, endless weeks of work and going back to my empty, lifeless apartment... it just seems so miserable now."

"Dang," Thomas whispers. "I'm actually not sure what to say. What about the Menendez Group project and the merger?"

I rest on my back again and stare up at the ceiling. "Honestly," I say with an ironic little laugh, "I don't care that much."

With a simple nod, Thomas rises from the corner of the bed. "Seems like your priorities have shifted," he says. "I think that's good, actually. I mean, we're all workaholics, but you have always been the worst one."

THOMAS LEFT SEVERAL MINUTES AGO, AND I CAN'T MAKE MYSELF PUT another thing in my suitcase. I've started with my workout clothes and two suits, but as soon as I'm about to put my new jeans in, I freeze. Something in my mind fires off, telling me to stop. I haven't felt this at odds with myself since deciding to leave Nebraska and move to New York to dedicate myself to work.

I wish I had talked to my dad about it back then....

Sliding out my phone, I find my father's contact and push the video message button. It rings three times, and his pixelated face comes up. His voice sounds garbled for a second, but I can still make out his words. "My son! What are you up to?"

There might be better service by the window, so I walk over and lean against it. I hold the phone in front of me, and my dad's face clears up. He looks older than I remember, with deeper lines on his forehead and patchy gray stubble around his chin. But somehow, his eyes are still bright. They remind me of Autumn and the way she looks when she's giving tours or watching ducks shimmy as they get out of the water.

"Hey, Dad." My throat constricts. "How are you?"

"Trisha!" my dad calls over his shoulder. "Our boy is on the phone!"

Hearing my mother's name brings up some long-forgotten emotion, and next thing I know, my eyes are brimming wet. I shift the phone away for a second and wipe at my face.

God, I've missed them so much. Why haven't I spoken to them in so long?

"Oh, Lukas!" Mom says, her face peeking over my father's arm.

Her hair is still blonde, but it's gotten a bit sandier, with some of the grays taking over. "It's so nice to hear from you!"

I let my face fall back into the frame. "I thought it was overdue," I explain.

"Where are you?" she asks, pointing behind me. "Or is this one of those green screen thingies?"

I chuckle, amazed she's ever heard the term 'green screen.' "I'm… in Vermont on a work trip."

"Really!" Dad exclaims. "That's quite the view!"

I turn around to see the scene I've memorized over the past month, the colorful array of trees surrounding the basin of the mountain. The dark, still water reflects the trees perfectly until a goose swims across or a fish comes up to nab a bug on the surface. It's like this view has become the screensaver for my brain somehow.

"Yeah," I say. "It is."

Mom scrunches her eyebrows together. "What's going on, honey? You look a little sad or something. Missing the city?"

It's funny how wrong she is. "Not at all, actually."

"Oh?" my parents both say at the same time.

I tell them everything, starting with more than two months ago when I was working twelve or fourteen-hour days and surviving off protein shakes and pre-made rotisserie chicken. I tell them how I went from dreading this trip to dreading the return to New York. I tell them about Autumn and how her hair is the perfect shade of auburn and her eyes are so bright and her laugh is so clear and contagious. I tell them about Maple Falls and how much I've come to love it: the scenery, the people, the sense of community, the little bits of history and the stories behind random things like the Kissing Bridge.

I learn from my parents that they're doing well, but my dad had been warned about taking care of his heart, that the doctor and my mother keep telling him to relax and stop working so much. It's ironic that even hundreds of miles away, I've managed to become a lot like him. It's not a bad thing, though, I realize.

Then I tell them something I didn't even know how to tell myself.

"I think you'd like it here. It reminds me of home," I say. "The good parts, you know, before I left."

Dad cocks his head. "What do you mean, son?"

That urgent emotion comes up again and bites up my throat. "I'm sorry," I say.

"What, honey? Why?" Mom asks.

I shrug. "I don't know. I just feel like... I ran away from home because I thought I could do better. I think I looked down on you guys for a long time because all I saw was the work and the struggle. I was so focused on eating the same meal for the whole winter or not being able to afford air conditioning that I thought you... that you had failed."

I hate myself for saying those words. I hate that they were true.

Dad has lost the shine in his eyes, but he doesn't look mad. "Lukas," he says, his voice deep and soothing. "I'm sorry you ever felt that way. I didn't realize our lacking those things hurt you so much."

I shake my head. "No, Dad, that's not the point. The point is I was wrong, and I'm sorry. I left home to look for success and happiness but wound up creating my own kind of stagnant version of a successful life. What you and Mom gave me, the good times and the memories, that's success. I just wish I had realized it sooner."

After talking with my parents for almost two hours, I manage to get some more items packed. I feel a little better, but thoughts of Autumn keep nagging at me. I want to talk to her about it, about this minor revelation I've had... but she's mad at me, and I don't fully understand why.

A couple of weeks ago, I was sure that our feelings were mutual. I had started picturing us going on more dates together and testing out what it might be like to be a couple.

A knock sounds at the door, and whoever it is starts to push it open before I even respond. I'm expecting Thomas, or maybe even

Branden, but it's neither. A pair of stiletto-heeled feet make their way through my doorway, shutting the door behind her.

Julia walks straight over and plops down right next to me, hip to hip.

I scoot away from her. "What are you doing here?"

"I came to help you pack. I heard you've been having trouble," she teases.

It falls flat on me. I'm not in the mood for joking, especially not with her.

"I don't know why it's so hard for you," she says, reaching out to put her hand on my knee. "I couldn't pack fast enough! I'm just so ready to get out of this annoying little town."

A spark of protection ignites in my chest. "Well, I like it here," I say. "I'd stay my whole life if I could."

Julia scoffs. "Yeah, right."

She thinks I'm joking. And even though I just said it off the cuff, I realize that what I just said might be true.

"What?" she says, her smile falling. "You're not serious, are you?"

I give a shrug with one shoulder and stand. "Maybe I am."

"Or maybe you need to get back to real like where you belong. This place–" She gestures out the window. "Is a dump. You're just dizzy from all the extra oxygen or something."

I shake my head. "I don't think so," I tell her. "I'm pretty sure I've never had a clearer mind. I like this place, these people."

Julia stands abruptly, glaring up at me. "These people?" she asks in disbelief. "What? Like that little Podunk tour guide?"

When I don't deny it, she smacks her lips and groans. "You have got to be kidding me."

"I'm not kidding you, and I'm not kidding myself. I would stay here longer… I want to stay here longer."

She changes tactics, stepping close to me and rubbing my arms up and down with both of her hands. "Lukas, how long is it going to take you to see that you have everything you need in New York? That you have everything you need… right here?"

My face twists into a grimace. "No, Julia," I tell her firmly, shrugging out of her hands. "There's nothing for me in New York. But you might be right. Almost anything I could ask for can be found here… in Maple Falls."

I start to turn around, but she catches me again and draws close. "Lukey…."

"Stop that!" I say. "It's one thing to touch my arm or call me stupid names I never liked, to follow me around and whatever once in a while, but this has got to stop. You can't keep hanging on me like this. Whatever you think happened that night three years ago is all in your head."

"But you… were going to kiss me. You helped me get away from those men, and you took me home… and you were just about to plant a kiss. I know you were," she says.

"What?" I run my hands through my hair with exasperation. "Is that what you think happened?" I can't believe she thought that all this time. "I got you away from them because they were bad news. I did it as a friend. I had no intention of kissing you or anything of the sort!"

Julia steps toward me again with her lips pursed and her eyes closed. I dodge her, exasperated, and take several steps back to put plenty of space between us.

"You need to go," I tell her firmly.

Julia glowers. "You'll regret it if you go after her," she says.

"I could never regret a moment with Autumn." I storm over to the door and open it so Julia can leave.

CHAPTER 19

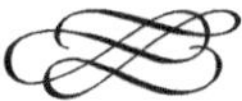

I couldn't help myself, so I got information from Ivy yesterday about Lukas's departure time. Now all I can do is think about how the time between now and then is quickly disappearing. He's leaving tomorrow, and I'm still stuck between being angry at him and wanting to see him just one more time.

I haven't seen him since I grumbled that goodbye, and I've felt awful ever since. I just... didn't want to believe that he had been stringing me along. I don't think I do believe that truly. But isn't it easier than saying goodbye to someone you've grown to care about and think of every minute of the day?

Maybe it's for the best, either way. Because wasn't it bound to end one way or another? I'm just ripping off the bandaid... at least, I think that's what I'm doing. Except, now it feels more like I ripped it off almost all of the way, and now it's painfully hanging on by a few last little hairs and I can't make myself finish the job.

Today, all the tour buses are helping assist the school in getting the kids to activities across the fairgrounds. It's the day before the

Autumn Leave Celebration, and it's a special time we save for the kiddos. They'll get free range in the mazes and the toned-down version of the haunted houses, as well as getting the first spin on the hayride that travels through town. It's a pretty huge event, and usually I find it so much fun.

This year feels a little bittersweet, though.

To my surprise, this morning Mr. Seeley asked me to follow him around to see how the operation runs from the management side of things. It caught me off guard, so I've just been following him around and taking notes, not really sure why he asked me specifically. Well… maybe it's because he knows how much I love this job. I wonder if he isn't sizing me up for a promotion of some kind, and the thought makes me feel sort of queasy.

I'd love nothing more than to dedicate all of my working hours to this job and maybe even get a raise in the process. But if he's looking at me for that, it means he's gotten even closer to retirement, and I don't think I'm ready for that. This place has always belonged to Mr. Seeley, and I can't picture it under other management.

"What do you think?" he asks when he shows me the plan for the tour on paper.

I hesitate to take the spreadsheets from him. They look so clean and organized. "Well, as you know, herding kids isn't much different from herding cats," I say with a laugh. "I think you've given plenty of time for each stop while managing time for loading and unloading the bus in between. Of course, I'm sure you've done this so many times, any plan you have is flawless."

Mr. Seeley clasps his hands behind his back and doesn't budge when I try to hand him the paper back. I look at him with confusion, and he only grins his toothy smile back at me. "Autumn, I'll be honest with you. I trust you more than anyone else on our team. We've got great workers, but you're the most dedicated, and there's no question that you love this more than anyone else."

I'm not sure where he's going with this, so I just nod slowly, trying not to let my skepticism show on my face.

"If you're up for it, I'd like to ease you into a more important role," he tells me.

"More important role?" I repeat.

He nods.

"I'm sorry, but what do you mean? What is this role?" I ask.

Mr. Seeley tugs on his navy blue ball cap. "I'll let you decide what to call it, Autumn. You can take it as far as you want to."

I wish that his answer cleared everything up for me, but it only makes me more confused. He seems to take note of this and wraps a spindly arm around my shoulders and gives me a squeeze.

"Just enjoy the day," he says, looking out at the tour buses, which are filling with children as we speak. "Think about it while you're leading this big day. Okay?"

I'm pretty sure my mouth is gaping open, and I'm totally bemazed. Befuddled? Amazed?

Fortunately, kicking off a giant tour with hundreds of kids take my mind off all the unpinned questions floating in my mind. I get to work helping the teachers and parent chaperones get organized while also managing a couple of newer staff members.

I do my best to be a jolly, happy, gleeful Autumn as I explain the itinerary to my busful of kids and teachers. They appear to be mostly third-graders, which is a fun age to work with. Kids that age are curious and excited while also–usually–maintaining that desire to please you and do what's right. They listen and join in when I help them memorize a chant about fall. I can't say I'm jealous of Marlene, who is matched with the fifth graders, who are notorious for leaving you to sing by yourself while silently and not-so-silently judging you.

The first stop is the high school football field, which has been decked out with a few fun games like the three-legged race, a little obstacle course, and a few others. We stay here for an hour and a half, spending fifteen minutes on each activity and using the five minutes in between to switch groups. This part is mostly up to the teachers and chaperones, but I watch closely and help where I can.

"Lukas, you're with this group!" one teacher yells, and she waves to a kid.

Of course, that name brings my mind to a screeching halt. Now my mind keeps replaying it.

Lukas....

I try to shake it off as we move on to the next stop: the apple orchard! We take the kids to a part of the orchard that we leave untouched for this specific event so they're still able to pick some fresh apples. This is also where the hayride begins and where my buddies Cally and Ivy are waiting to meet up with me.

They keep me company while the kids are on their hayrides, and, of course, they're both asking me how I'm doing with the heartbreak situation.

"I'm not heartbroken," I tell them. "That's too dramatic. I'm... I'm just hurt. There's a difference."

Cally presses her lips together, clearly wanting to correct me but not wanting to risk pushing my buttons.

We're sitting on the porch of the orchard's little mercantile, where their gift shop and bakery is located. The smell of fresh apple turnovers and sweet pear bread wafts through every time someone opens the door.

"I haven't seen him much in the last couple of weeks," Ivy chimes in. "I ran into him a couple of times when he was out for runs and stuff. It seems like everyone else meets in the common room, but I haven't seen him at all this week."

My chest tightens, and Cally seems to sense it. She squeezes my arm lightly. "He's probably locked up in his room or something," I mutter. "It seems like that was his way of life back in New York."

Ivy continues. "And I saw him and that blonde girl fi—"

Cally gives her a stern look and stops her mid-sentence. "Why don't we go get some baked goods?" she says instead.

I know she's trying to protect me by avoiding the conversation, but I actually like hearing someone else talk about Lukas. And I wonder what she was going to say about Julia.

It's silly, I know, to obsess about this when I've only gone on two dates with the guy. But I know he's going back, and no matter what, I do want him to be happy. It would have been nice if we could have spent more time together, that I could have gotten to experience more of him, but....

I shake my head and stand. "It's almost time for the next thing," I say. "See you guys in a couple of hours?"

They both nod. Cally is looking at me with poorly masked pity, and Ivy looks like she feels guilty for bringing up Julia. I give them my best reassuring smile and head back to the bus.

AFTER LUNCH AND YET ANOTHER BUS RIDE BACK TO THE CITY CENTER with the kiddos, we make our final stop. It's like a soft-opening for the festival where the kids are free to explore and some of their parents join us as we partake in some more activities. Now is the time for the kids to do the real fun, crucial fall activities, like bobbing for apples and learning how to bake pies. There are a lot of helpers at each station and tent, including my aunt and Cally's mom.

Ivy is manning the tent where kids are bobbing for apples to win prizes. Cally's mom is helping a small group of older kids make pies in the kitchen of the restaurant. And Cally has joined me at the pumpkin carving station. Aunt Bev is very close, doing a sort of DIY wreath making class with a group. The day is nice as I look around. It's perfect fall weather, and the sun is shining, but I feel like something is missing.

"Is it pathetic to wonder what Lukas is doing right now?" I ask. "You're probably tired of me whining about this, but I'm almost done, I promise. Just give me...." I want to say another day or another week, but I don't really think I'd be telling her the truth if I do. "A little more time."

Cally helps a girl make a moon-shaped eye. "I think," she says slowly to me, "you're the only one who knows how deeply you've been hurt or disappointed, and you're the only one who knows when you're healed. So take whatever time you need, and I'll be here."

I smile. It's a little on the sad side, but it's there.

After the day is over, my Aunt Bev and Cally take me to the Maple Falls Café, and we have a couple of hot cocoas and appetizers. I try my best to stay involved and engaged in the conversation, but I keep catching sight of the clock, which is getting closer and closer to midnight.

"What is it, dear?" Aunt Bev asks, patting my leg. "You've been staring at the clock all night. You wanna head home?"

The last thing I really want is to be alone. I'd drown in these Lukas thoughts for sure if I was....

"No," I say.

She gives me a knowing look, urging me to be honest.

"Fine," I say. "In twelve minutes... it'll be tomorrow. And tomorrow he's leaving. He'll be on a plane with his snotty blonde girlfriend heading back to New York, and I'll be here wishing was with me instead."

I hadn't expected to confess this out loud. Maybe it's the super rich cocoa. I take another drink of it anyway, even though it's become lukewarm.

"Oh, baby girl," my aunt says with a sigh, wrapping both her arms around me and squeezing me against her. "You really got it bad, didn't you?"

Thanks to the cocoa and auntie hug mix, tears boil over. "I'm just ready for tomorrow to be over with so I can move on."

CHAPTER 20

Even though I knew it was coming, I'm not prepared for today. I tossed and turned all night, and I even called my parents at 2:00 A.M. when I couldn't sleep. To my surprise, my dad answered. His sleepy voice still seemed overjoyed to hear from me for the second time in less than a week.

I told him I was sorry and that I planned to call more often and maybe even come down for a visit. We chatted in hushed tones for a couple of hours about my job and about the farm. He asked me about Autumn, and I told him I was sure I liked her, but I wasn't sure what would happen. The truth is, I just didn't want to admit my defeat. If I left it open-ended and let my dad believe something good might come out of it, then it sort of means that it keeps my hope alive, too, even if that is a cruel thing to do to myself.

Now, I'm standing in the middle of my room thinking the same thing over and over again. My plane leaves today. This is it. This is the end. I'm not ready.

I'm leaving Maple Falls, Vermont, first thing this morning, in a couple of hours, actually. I'm leaving Autumn. Somehow, I manage to pack my suitcase the rest of the way, though I'm not sure having Thomas and Miles shove everything in in less than five minutes is considered packing.

The two of them drag me out to the front porch of the inn. Branden is giving some lame team talk to us from the lawn while Ivy and her father stand awkwardly behind him, waiting to say their formal thank yous and farewells. I think that Ivy keeps glancing at me, but every time I almost meet her eyes, she looks away. I know she and Autumn are friends, and I wonder if she knows something. I consider stepping away to talk in private, but before I can make a move, she thanks us and runs off, literally.

Suspicious….

After Mr. Dear thanks us again and encourages us to leave an honest review about the place on their website, Branden steps up, thanks him, and launches into another teamwork spiel.

"You know we're going to be together forever," Miles teases. "It's not like we're saying our final goodbyes. We're just leaving this place, traveling together for the next four to five hours, and we'll be seeing each other in the office in a couple of days."

The rest of the team laughs, but I can't.

Be together forever? My stomach sinks. I don't think I want that. I don't want to be part of Fin-vice forever.

Our final goodbyes? I don't want that either. My chest tightens and twists. I don't want to say goodbye to Autumn at all.

The group moves toward the shuttle, but I'm not ready. I turn around and take a good look at the inn. I see the trails that wrap around the property and wind through the mountains and past the lake where I ran nearly every morning. It was so much better than running in the park across from my apartment. The give of the soft earth under my feet and the occasional crunch of dry leaves and twigs sure beat the hard thudding of my tennis shoes on the paved side-walk, dodging discarded food and cracks that could roll an ankle.

Through the window, I see Luis cooking. He'd learned my favorite omelet after the first three times and even started specializing it for me. I see the bit of woods that separates the event building from the inn where Autumn and I officially ran into each other and hit it off instantly. I remember how stunned she looked when she ran into me and how relieved she was when she realized I wasn't a bear, how her laugh sounded as we teased each other and got to know each other as we carried the punch through the dim night.

That night led to two of the best days of my whole life, my dates with her. I wish I could have had a thousand more dates with Autumn, a thousand more reasons to see her smile. I wish I could learn a thousand more things about her and tell her a thousand more times how absolutely lovely I think she is.

It was all too perfect for too short a time. There's no way it was all my imagination. I couldn't have made up these feelings, and I couldn't have dreamed up the way she looked at me. Right...?

I feel a hand on my shoulder. "We've gotta get going, Lukas," Thomas tells me with a low voice. He gently urges me to turn around, and we get on the shuttle to take to the airport.

I can't help but notice how happy everyone looks to be leaving, dressed in their suits again and chatting cheerily with each other. They're probably talking about the exciting changes going on in the company, but I know it all means even more late nights of work. Julia is somber, but I know how much she hates this place, so there's no question what she's thinking. Even Branden, who was perhaps the most excited person to be going on this trip, seems like he's so eager to get back home—though I think his excitement might be exhaustion induced. On any other day, I'd probably find his sleepy smile kind of funny. I know how much work it takes to make a bunch of Type As relax. I wonder what Autumn's plan for us would be on a similar vacation. If we all spent a couple hours with her, I'm sure everyone would be coaxed into sweaters and knit hats in no time... except maybe Julia....

I can't match the excited chatter as I sink into my seat and Christopher asks what I think we should do as soon as we get back.

I grunt and mutter something about getting back on the plane for round two. He must think it's a joke, but Julia hears it another way.

"What is your problem?" she asks. "Why are you so hung up on this stupid place?"

I ignore her and ask Thomas to switch seats with me so I can be closer to the window. I want to take advantage of it. As we wind through the trees, I try to catch every color and commit it to memory, especially the red-brown that reminds me of her hair and the little traces of green clinging onto some of the leaves that remind me of her eyes. We go over the cerulean Kissing Bridge, and I wish that Autumn and I could have gone there together, alone. I would have put together a little picnic, and she would have told me the story of her aunt and uncle's engagement. Maybe we would have even shared a kiss....

Time is going by too quickly. The closer we get to the airport, the more nauseous I feel.

"You okay?" Thomas asks as we step off the shuttle and onto the airport sidewalk.

"I don't know," I reply.

At the airport, I follow the group like a zombie, my eyes fixed mindlessly on the heels of Thomas's shoes as he walks in front of me. As we're standing in line to check our bags, my phone buzzes in my pocket. I almost ignore it, but it goes off again.

There's nothing else to do in this line other than wait, so I pull it out of my pocket and my heart rate spikes.

It's a text. From Autumn.

Regardless of the outcome, I've decided I'm glad I met you, the first message reads. Then, right under that, *I just wanted you to know.*

There's a sense of finality in these messages that I can't ignore... and I can't accept.

I'm still in a daze when Julia bumps me from behind. "It's your turn. Pay attention."

I didn't even know she's been behind me this whole time.

"Lukas," Thomas calls from ahead of me. "It's time."

Yes, I think. It is time. Time to take a risk.

I stoop down to the floor and splay open my rolling suitcase. I rustle through until I find all the sweaters that Autumn helped me pick out. Shaking out all the contents of my small duffle bag, I shove the sweaters in there along with a couple other necessities, throwing the rest back into my suitcase.

Everyone is probably looking at me like I'm crazy. Heck, I might actually be crazy.

"What in the world are you doing?" Julia asks, clearly annoyed.

I smile up at her. "None of your business," I say.

"Why do you want with those? Throwing them in the trash where they belong?" she says callously.

I ignore her and zip up my duffle bag before slinging it over my shoulder. The people at the counter don't seem like they want to wait for me, so they take my rolling suitcase and heft it behind the counter. It disappears down the conveyor belt, and as it gets farther away, my chest feels brighter and brighter.

I catch Thomas's expression as I turn to leave. He's wearing a strange, shocked half-smile. I shrug and return his look with the first genuine smile I've worn in weeks. I take off past the other people in line, apologizing to all the shoulders my duffle bag hits on the way out. Julia and Branden are calling after me, but as their voices fade away I find a strange sense of peace.

There's no telling what's going to happen, one way or the other, but all I know is that I can't get on that plane. There are other things I need to do. Things I want to do.

My walk is brisk, and my hands are shaking with adrenaline. I pull out my phone to make a couple of calls.

CHAPTER 21

TODAY'S THE BIG DAY, MY MOST FAVORITE DAY OF THE WHOLE YEAR. YET, my mood is more sour than ever. I wake up late, feeling groggy and agitated. Tess is whimpering at me to take her outside, so I slide on my slip-on suede clogs and pull over an oversized sweatshirt and some sweatpants. I know Lukas is about to board his plane. He could already be on it... and something has been nagging at me.

I nibble on my lip, weighing my options. Meanwhile, Tess zigzags from side to side on the sidewalk. Everything my aunt said to me is still bouncing around in my head. Things like "you can't deny what's in front of you even if it's bound to leave you" and "magic is magic no matter how long it lasts." So I make a decision, the first real decision I've made since deciding not to see Lukas again. I send him a text.

Regardless of the outcome, I've decided I'm glad I met you.

It's true, even though I'm upset that I saw him with Julia and even more upset at the fact that he's leaving in general—and maybe a little upset that he didn't try harder to see me, although I guess I didn't make that part too easy. Despite all of that, this is the first time I felt hope. It's also the first time I felt despair, or at least something akin to it.

The message seems out of the blue because it is. Part of me hopes he doesn't see it until he lands. Part of me hopes he doesn't see it at all. It's a little embarrassing, but I feel like it's necessary. If I can't admit my feelings, then I can't accept the hurt and I can't move past it. This is just… part of the process to get over him.

But it doesn't make me feel better right away.

It's still a little early in the morning, but outside the sun is too bright and the air is too soft and breezy. I hear the gentle rustling of the tree leaves overhead that's too soothing. Even though I'm blocks away, I can still smell the familiar fresh cinnamon fragrance of baked goods, and those are comforting. It's too perfect of a day to be ruined.

I know I'm avoiding the day, avoiding reality. Nothing will change now. All I have to do is get through it. The disappointment and the tight squeeze in my chest will pass, eventually. I just have to take it one day at a time, one hour at a time. It just so happens that spending an hour sleeping in bed is easier than walking around out in the happy world when you're feeling the opposite. So I crawl back into bed and bury myself under the covers.

I wake up again a couple of hours later. Nervously, I peek at my phone. There is only one message from my aunt. Any bit of hope I was clinging onto fizzles out. I lay my phone face down inside a drawer and shut it away. Out of sight, out of mind…

It's after ten. Lukas's plane is long gone by now. He's probably getting close to New York. I grit my teeth. "He doesn't even like it there," I mutter to myself.

Outside, I'm sure everyone is starting to fill the streets of the festival already, getting in the early shopping at the booths or picking up a sweet treat for breakfast. I consider crawling back into bed, but my door opens and Aunt Bev prances through. She's wearing her hair in a cute messy bun and she's got a long scarf draped around her neck. She's holding two cups of coffee and grinning at me like a maniac.

"What?" I groan.

She shoves the coffee into my hand. "Drink up, my dear. It's Autumn Leaves Celebration Day, your favorite day of the year!"

I set the coffee on my dresser. "I don't want—"

"You'll regret it if you don't go," she says sternly. It surprises me a bit because she rarely uses that voice on me. I think she would have made a very scary, loving mother if she and Uncle Henry would have had children. "Enough moping. I am not going to let you ruin your favorite day of the year."

I'm just standing there with my arms sagging at my sides, never feeling more lifeless.

"Whether it's in a couple of days, a couple of weeks, a couple of months, or even three hundred sixty-five days from now, I know you'll regret not going out there today," she tells me.

I nod my head. "Okay," I sigh. Maybe I don't have the gall to argue with her or maybe I think she's right. Either way, I tug on a pair of jeans, a purple sweater, and my clogs. She brushes my hair and adds a touch of concealer under my eyes.

Ivy and Cally take over dragging me through the festival. I can't will my feet to go any faster with them than I did for the last couple of hours with Aunt Bev. She abandoned me to take care of some business, something about checking on the shop and then preparing a treat for later.

"You want to ride the Ferris wheel?" Ivy asks, tugging on my arm. The little Ferris wheel is the only ride other than the hay ride.

"Sure," I say. I don't want to ruin their good time, and I appreciate that they're doing their best to cheer me up, so I find it hard to deny anything either of them suggests.

"I was thinking about adding hot-air balloon rides next year," Cally tells us when we're slowly rotating in circles.

"That would be cool," I say. It does sound fun.

"Yeah!" Ivy agrees. "I think that would be totally popular! It's probably expensive though…."

They chat a little more about the ideas, and we move on to the next thing. They've almost worn me down, and it cheers me up a little when we go through the haunted house and Cally screams so loud that the worker is actually concerned. It elicits a giggle from me and a torrent of laughs from Ivy.

But when we're almost to the end, we catch up to a cute couple who are walking through hand in hand, the girl hiding slightly behind the boy's shoulder. I feel a tug in my chest, wondering how Lukas would feel about going through a haunted house. I think he might secretly be afraid, but he'd put up a front to protect whoever he's with.

When we exit, Ivy looks disturbed, not by the haunted house, but by me because tears are falling down my face.

She and Cally hug me on both sides. "I'm sorry," Cally says. "We should have given you more time. We can go back to your house if you want."

Ivy is rubbing my back and looks like she's about to cry, too.

"This is so ridiculous," I say. "I've never felt so ridiculous."

Both of my friends are quiet as they comfort me and let me cry for a couple of minutes. The concealer my aunt made me wear is now useless.

"It's ridiculous how I could fall for a guy after two dates," I start. "It's ridiculous how I can be so attached to him after I saw him with another woman. It's ridiculous how I'm pining over him when I know he's already back in New York, where he thinks he belongs. And it's ridiculous that I think he could possibly belong here."

"I guess it's not the kind of magic you expected," Cally says. "But all this unexplainable so-called ridiculous stuff sure points to some kind of magic, huh?"

"Or a curse," I laugh.

"How cruel," Ivy says sadly, lying her head on my shoulder.

I suck in a deep breath and wipe away the dampness on my face.

"Let's go," I say. When Cally starts walking back to my house, I pull her back. "No. Not home. I want a cinnamon cider."

She smiles at me and nods. Together, the three of us walk through the festival with our pinkies hooked together. We're an odd assortment of sadness at this fun and upbeat festival.

A little later, two of Cally's little cousins find us. They're all dressed up in their princess and train conductor costumes, and they look great.

"You guys are so cute," Ivy says, patting Meena on her slicked-back hair.

Meena curtsies. "Thank you for helping make these," she says to me and Cally. She hugs us quickly. "Do you want to come carve pumpkins with us?"

My two friends look at me, and I nod. We join the kids at the corner of the festival, where a large tent covers a row of tables with jack-o'-lanterns and untouched pumpkins. We all choose a pumpkin each and grab the carving supplies and sit in the middle on a tarp. Cally places an apron over my head to protect my clothes and does the same for her cousins. "You all better not get those awesome costumes dirty, or I'll hire a ghost to haunt you."

My heart isn't in it, but I make an attempt. Gravity and sadness keep pulling my hands down though, so my pumpkin is looking rather frowny. He looks about as pathetic as I feel.

"That's an awfully sad pumpkin for a woman named Autumn," a voice says behind me.

The hairs on my neck spike up along with my heartbeat.

It can't be....

I slowly turn around, and Lukas is standing there in his charcoal-colored sweater and jeans, smiling softly at me.

First, I want to jump up and run over to him. I had secretly been wondering what it might have felt like for him to hold me... but then I remember everything else and I turn back around.

"Autumn," he pleads. "Don't turn away from me. Please, let's just talk."

I'm looking frantically between Cally and Ivy. They're equally shocked by Lukas's appearance. Meanwhile, Meena and Jack are obliviously carving away at their pumpkins.

I hear his footsteps coming up slowly behind me. It makes my stomach sink and my spine shiver. My body is betraying me....

"Autumn," he whispers. He's standing next to me now, so close to me that I almost feel the air move with his voice.

My head turns on its own to look over at him. His dark, cavernous eyes are desperate and hopeful. I want to climb in there and curl up for hibernation like a black bear. I want to make a home in those eyes.

"Autumn," he says again, so quietly, just for me. And in the way that he says my name, I can sense something... an unexplainable, a powerful, supernatural force that makes me give in.

"Okay," I say. I almost don't hear myself.

Lukas gently removes the pumpkin from my lap and sets it on the ground beside Cally. He gingerly pulls the apron over my head and uses a damp towel from the table to wipe off my hands. All I can do is let it happen, and all the while my body is growing warmer, my skin is alive with prickles and pulses. I'm watching his face, serene and focused on my hands. His touch is gentle and easy. I feel so cared for, it makes me momentarily forget why I was so mad at him in the first place....

"Wait," I say, pulling my hand away and gulping down the hope swelling in my throat. "Let's just... talk first."

CHAPTER 22

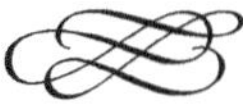

*L*ᴜᴋᴀs*

Wᴀᴛ ʜᴜʀᴛs ᴍᴏʀᴇ ᴛʜᴀɴ ᴡᴀᴛᴄʜɪɴɢ Aᴜᴛᴜᴍɴ's ᴅᴇʟɪɢʜᴛ ᴀᴛ sᴇᴇɪɴɢ ᴍᴇ morph into a frown matching her sad pumpkin, is the way she pulls her hand away from me. Granted, I didn't expect to take her hands like this, and so suddenly. After all, I've been in her presence for less than two minutes, and I haven't seen her in over two weeks. And I take it she wasn't expecting me to be here, despite the voicemails I left her.

Maybe she really doesn't want to see me. I thought that text she sent might have been my last chance to salvage whatever beautiful thing we'd started, but maybe it was just her way of saying goodbye.

I follow her to the sidewalk, where a few tables are set up outside. I note the way her shoulders are slumped and her footsteps seem slow and tired. She sits at the farthest empty table. Rather than sit across from her, I place myself beside her with a respectable distance between us, and angle myself in her direction.

Her hands are in her lap again, like that morning we went to Cascade, our second date, the day that everything changed.

"What happened?" I ask.

She looks down at her hands. Her feet fidget.

I rephrase the question and refrain from reaching out to touch her hands. "What's wrong, Autumn? Why won't you even look at me?"

Her eyes flick over to me briefly and then back down. "I thought you'd be back in New York by now."

I clench my hand into a fist, willing all my self-restraint there. "I'm not going back," I say.

Her feet stop moving. Her eyes slowly shift over to me. She's wary.

"I realized," I say, sucking in a breath. Excitement builds up in me, and it's so hard not to blurt out everything I've realized in the last couple of days and especially in the last several hours. "I want to stay here, in Maple Falls."

Autumn's lips part as if to say something, but she stops herself. I wait patiently, as patiently as I can. Finally, her face changes again. It's back to anger. "What about work? What about Julia?"

"What?" I ask, confused. "What about Julia?"

Autumn huffs but doesn't raise her voice. "You said she wasn't your girlfriend, and then I saw you two together on a date. You looked awfully cozy that night. You said I was... that she wasn't...."

I'm searching her face for answers. Past her pinched-together eyebrows and her trembling lips, I can see pieces of the puzzle falling together. I'd never once been on a date with Julia, and there was never a situation that could have possibly been misconstrued that way. But then I remember it, the night I went with Julia to have dinner in town, and the way she was acting that night. It made sense now.

"Autumn," I say, bowing my head to catch her eyes when she starts to look away again. "I promise you, I've never been on a date with Julia. I know what night you're talking about, though. Yes, we were together, eating dinner, but I assure you, it wasn't a date."

The answer isn't good enough. Autumn is still staring at me like she isn't sure she can trust me.

"It's no excuse, though," I continue. "For a long time, Julia has been attached to me. I never stopped her because... well, I felt kind of bad for her. I didn't know where to draw the line and I thought she was harmless. But during this trip, I started to realize her intentions. Believe me, I put a stop to it. She hasn't stopped glaring at me for days now."

I think I see some of the anger die away when Autumn's mouth twitches up. She corrects it though. She's not convinced just yet.

"That night, she said she wanted to get away from the inn. I did, too. After all, I'd been moping because a certain someone suddenly started giving me the cold shoulder." I pause to see how it's going, and she's still got her eyes trained on me. Seems like a win, so I keep going. I want her to know the truth. "Julia said we should have dinner and even explicitly said that it's not a date. That's the only reason I agreed. Plus, I was planning on surprising you afterward at your house...."

"Why didn't you?" she asks quietly.

Such a simple question is like a harmonious chorus of angels to my ears. "I was afraid of making things worse, I think," I admit. "Everything is so new between us. I didn't know if you needed time. Plus, I wasn't even sure why you'd become angry with me. I didn't have a plan for once. I didn't know what to do."

Autumn blinks at me. "So it wasn't a date? And you really aren't seeing her?"

My heart is swelling so much I think it'll burst out of my chest. "It wasn't, and I'm not. I thought she was acting strangely, scooting up next to me. Now I know she was doing that on purpose because she must have seen you. I never have wanted to and I never will want to date Julia. I just want...." I'm still afraid of pushing too much too fast, so I let the words fall away and hope that she can feel my sincerity, that all I want is her.

She takes a deep breath in and out. "And... you think you want to stay here? In Maple Falls?"

I shake my head. "No. I know that I want to stay here."

"But what about your job?"

I shrug. "I realize that I don't care. Two dates with you were enough to help me realize how many joys in life I've missed out on while I've been glued to my desk and my useless goals. I just want to enjoy my life, to take each day slowly, to go on little and big adventures, to relish in the little things."

Autumn shifts, coming a bit closer to me. Worried I might spook her away like a butterfly on a flower, I remain still, just watching. "I was scared, too," she admits. "That's why I pulled away from you."

My fingers twitch with the desire to touch her face. Just wait a little while longer, I coach myself silently.

"When you said you were excited to go back to New York but also that you were having fun with me… I felt like that meant I was just a way to pass the time or something." She sighs and picks at her fingernails. "I wasn't really angry until later, when I saw you with Julia. Just when I was starting to accept my feelings for you… even if we weren't going to get a lot of time together… I saw you two sitting like that, with her practically in your lap, and I used it as an excuse to keep my distance from you. I thought I misunderstood your intentions."

She braves a look at me. It's overwhelming, the sensation of putting my heart in her hands. "Then why don't I tell you my intentions?" I suggest, reaching out to grasp her fingers. They're cool from the fall air. She lets me take them up, which gives me enough confidence to keep going. "I want to spend as much time as humanly possible with you, to go on adventures with you, discover new places and new things about myself and about you. You see, I think I lost parts of myself when I chose to go to New York. I was trying to be successful and make a comfortable life for myself so I could avoid the life my parents had. They always worked too hard, and we never seemed to get ahead."

I take a breath. "But you… you helped me realize that you can't measure success and comfort the same way. You helped me to uncover a sense of peace, and that sense of peace carved a way to understanding my parents' lifestyle. They never wanted anything more than what they had. Despite the chores and labor, they were satisfied with their simple lives. I can't remember a time when they weren't happy." I realize this as I'm speaking, and it tugs at my heart. I want to hug my parents and apologize to them for taking our life for granted, for running away from some made up idea of success. "I don't know how I missed that, but I see it now... I want to discover more of that. And I want to do that with you by my side, if you'll have me."

"Lukas," she says slowly. I think she's going to pull away again. The stillness hangs heavy in the air as I wait for her to continue. "I want that, too."

I squeeze her fingers a bit tighter, and she finally turns to face me, our knees bumping together.

"Lukas," she says. My name never sounded better. "I think... I've been waiting for you for a long time, even before I met you. Somehow, you're nothing that I expected and everything I—"

Her face begins to glow with a bit of pink blush. Somehow I know what she's trying to tell me.

"Can we pick up where we left off?" I ask her, lifting her hand to my mouth and kissing her lightly on the knuckles. "You know, before I said that stupid thing about being excited to go back to New York?"

A soft, short giggle escapes her that makes my heart feel like it has sprouted wings. "Okay," she says. Then with a sigh, "I'm not going to pretend to understand all of this, but I don't want to waste any more time being afraid that it will end."

An uncontainable smile splits my face. "If I have any say, it won't end."

IT FEELS LIKE THE BEST KIND OF DREAM AS AUTUMN AND I WALK HAND in hand through the Autumn Leaves Celebration, well, hand in hand in my pocket. The evening is upon us, and the cool air rushes over the festival grounds, so I have captured Autumn's hand with mine and am caging it in my hoodie pocket. She doesn't seem to mind, occasionally squeezing my hand.

We stroll through the vendors and past the little activities. She tells me some more about Maple Falls and her life growing up here. Every word pours over me like soft, warm honey. I want to learn everything I can about Autumn, and I want to find my place in this little, cozy town. I want to find that new sense of home, and create that peace and contentment that my parents shared with each other.

"Hey! That's mine!" I say when we pass by the pottery tent. My pottery class instructor from the event building next to the inn, Mrs. Day, sits under the plastic awning with little shelves of clay vases and bowls surrounding her. Right on the front table with a few other pieces is a sign that reads: Pottery classes Wednesdays at 3:00 P.M.

I'm tugging Autumn up to the little display, feeling like a kid at a science fair, showing off my project.

"Which one is it?" Autumn asks with a laugh. "No, wait, let me guess."

She puts her free index finger to her chin and looks back and forth between me and the table of handmade treasures. There are about five different pieces, but somehow she magically guesses which is mine when she points to the wavy-edged bowl in the middle.

"What? How did you guess that?" I ask.

She shrugs and gives me a wink. My heart's newly sprouted wings give out temporarily, and it's free-falling blissfully.

"Do you want to keep it, Mr. Spellman?" Mrs. Day asks.

Autumn twists to me with an incredulous look on her face.

"What?" I ask, suddenly nervous.

The corner of her mouth tilts up. "Your last name is Spellman?"

I nod slowly. Funny how we never shared that, but it still felt like I knew her. "Why? You think it's funny?"

She shakes her head no, even though the grin on her face says yes. "It's just ironic, is all," she says, like I'm missing some inside joke.

"No, you keep it," I tell Mrs. Day. "I'll be back to make something better."

"So," Autumn says, sliding her free hand into my pocket where our hands are still clasped together. "What other talents should we uncover?"

"Something tells me I'd carve a pretty impressive pumpkin," I tease.

"Okay, then," Autumn laughs. She walks backward, pulling me after her, wearing a mischievous smile. "Let's make it a contest."

CHAPTER 23

"Did you call your parents?" I ask Lukas.

We've just met in the parking lot of the cathedral, the only place left to park thanks to the busiest day of the festival.

He immediately takes my hand and plants a kiss on the top of my head like it's the most natural thing in the world. He feels like a 'spell-man' to me. Everything he does shoots a magic spark through me.

"I did," he says into my hair. "They say they'd love to visit. They came to New York once, but it wasn't really their style. I think they'd like it here, though."

It's so surreal thinking that Lukas is planning to stay. He's giving up all of his hard work to be here. I have to say, however, that his dark, cavernous eyes have never seemed so full of light, and he's never seemed more comfortable than now, standing in a cozy sweater and jeans, walking across the street hand in hand with me.

"They should come in the spring. It's the second best time of the year here, when everything is turning green and the flowers are sprouting up," I tell him.

"And the cute little baby bears are traipsing through the woods learning how to scare people," Lukas says dreamily.

I scowl at him, and he taps my nose with his finger. "I'm kidding," he says. "I'm excited to see it all. Have you been camping out there before? In the woods, I mean."

I shake my head no. "Not since I was a kid, but… should we try it?"

"There's no one else I'd rather run into a bear with," he says.

"You're ridiculous," I tell him. But I love it.

The big Autumn Leaves Celebration is underway, with Main Street and the whole town square overrun with booths and tents and activities and food trucks. Quite literally the whole town must be out today. The air is buzzing with excitement and chatter. The smell of sweet baked goods mixes with other scents from warm fried goods and lingers in the air.

"This is delicious!" Lukas says after I have him try a Maple Falls special cinnamon cider for the first time.

"It's even better with this," I say, taking out a couple of candied walnuts from a little paper bag I'd bought earlier. He eats them out of my hand and moans with delight.

"That is a good pairing," he says after swallowing and taking another sip of cider. "I love this place."

Finally, we make it to the middle of Main Street, where my aunt's shop is located. I can see through the window that her shop is flooded with customers, and the line at the register is stretching through the entire store. I don't see her helper, but I do see Aunt Bev frantically scanning items for one customer and trying to answer questions for another.

"I think I better hop in there and help her out," I tell Lukas. He nods and follows me into the store. The music on the overhead speakers is drowned out by the murmur of customers.

"You want some help?" I ask Aunt Bev.

She looks totally relieved to see me. Her eyes flick to Lukas, who is standing behind me.

"I'd like to help, too, if that's okay," he says.

Aunt Bev smiles at us both. "Fine. Autumn is the best and quickest cashier in all the land. What are your skills?" She raises her eyebrows at Lukas.

"My first job was a bag boy at the supermarket," he says.

I grab him by the sleeve, pull him behind the counter with me, and quickly show him the paper bags and the tissue we use to wrap fragile items.

We quickly find our groove. I greet customers and scan their items before passing them off to Lukas, who expertly wraps and loads them into the paper bags. He makes small talk with other people, commenting on their purchases and asking them how they're enjoying the festival. I like seeing this side of him. It makes my heart feel abuzz like a hive of gentle worker bees.

We end up helping Aunt Bev for almost two hours before the traffic dies down, and she decides to close the shop for the rest of the evening. We share a moment with Aunt Bev at the back of the store, and I leave the two of them alone for a couple of minutes to go up and check on Tess. I bring her back down with me. She sniffs Lukas's leg before quickly deciding that she likes him and starts jumping up and licking his hand when he tries to pet her.

The three of us—well, four including Tess—take a stroll through the nearby park. It seems like Lukas and Aunt Beverly are getting along well, which makes me happy. They talk about baseball, and I learn that Lukas helped his team get to the state championships two times while he was in high school.

"Would you guys want to go to a game with me sometime?" Aunt Bev asks.

Her question catches me by surprise, considering the last time she tried to go she was too overcome with sadness that Henry wasn't there with her. I feel tears biting their way up to my eyes. "Are you sure?" I ask her.

She smiles softly and nods. "Yeah. I think it's time to try again. Maybe I don't have to go alone."

I wrap my aunt in a hug. "Of course you don't have to. I'd love to go."

Lukas seems a little lost, but he goes with the flow. "Yeah, it sounds like fun. Let's do it."

A little while later, Aunt Beverly offers to take Tess back home and tells me and Lukas to finish up the night on our own. We decide that we actually are a little hungry, and agree to part ways. Before we leave, my aunt hugs me and whispers in my hear that she's excited for me. She gives a hug to Lukas, too, which he returns a bit awkwardly. It's endearing though, and I find myself eager to have his hand in mine again.

"Halloween? Of course I loved Halloween at one point," Lukas tells me over a shared plate of cheesy fries at the Maple Falls Cafe. "Before I grew up and became distracted by work and success, I was just a regular boy who wanted to be a Power Ranger."

I cackle. "No way. Which one? Blue?"

"Red," he replies. "Everyone knows red is the best. The best flavor, the best color, the best hair…." His eyes wash over me.

I roll my eyes at his attempt to flirt, but it does cause my chest to feel light and fluttery.

"I lived in a small community that didn't exactly have a fall festival like this," he explains. "My mom took me to the next town over for trick-or-treating until I was about twelve, then I started wanting to hang out with my friends to watch scary movies… then I started wanting to grow up and became desperate to start my own life."

"Where you became a workaholic?" I tease.

Lukas shoots out a short and airy laugh. "Yeah, pretty much. Though I guess, looking at it now, I just transplanted the work ethic my dad instilled in me in a way I viewed as more successful."

"What made it more successful to you?" I ask.

He leans back into the booth. "I guess it was just the money. I thought we were poor because we lived such a simple life, but even in New York, I didn't really buy much."

"Just three hundred and sixty-five suits?"

"Not even ten suits, probably," Lukas laughs. Then he becomes a little more serious. "Maybe he took work a little too seriously some-times, but it's clear to me now that I did the same thing. I'm really glad I came here and realized that there's more to life than meeting goals and checking off lists." He finds my hand under the table and gives it a little squeeze.

"I'm glad you came here, too," I tell him.

Lukas smiles and pops a fry into his mouth with his unoccupied hand. "I like it here," he says. "I'd really like to stay."

I'm too happy to say anything, or maybe I don't say anything because I'm still trying to believe it all.

After dinner, we make our way around what's left of the festival. The night is getting cooler and dimmer, and some places are shutting down while others combat the lateness with string lights and exciting music.

We stop by every booth, only separating once when I have to go to the bathroom.

At the end of the night, we walk back to the church parking lot, where Lukas has parked his rental car. "Can I take you home?" he asks.

It's only a few blocks away from here, but I nod, pleased with any excuse to extend our time together. We ride quietly in the car, slowly making our way back across town. Lukas is playing some sort of easy listening pop music. In this moment, the night feels so perfect. I don't let myself worry about how things will work out.

Back at home, Lukas walks me to the door. He caresses my face softly, tucking my hair behind my ear. "I actually got you something," he practically whispers.

"What is it?" I ask.

He reaches into his pocket and pulls out a little cloth bag. He opens it and empties out its contents into his hand and puts the little bag back in his pocket. As he unfolds the necklace and holds it up, he says, "It made me think of you. And I just wanted you to have it."

The necklace is beautiful, with wispy leaves linked together like a whirlwind of fall. Each leaf is painted a bit differently, echoing the change in the leaves found on the trees–golden yellow, amber, and bronzy brown.

"This is so pretty," I say, touching it. I lift my hair and turn around so Lukas can fasten it around my neck. I feel his fingertips brush the nape of my neck and then gingerly gather my hair up and let it cascade down my back again.

When I turn back around, he is smiling at me. "You are so pretty," he replies.

I don't know why I'm compelled to ask, but the words slip out of my mouth before I can do anything to stop them. "So, we're really doing this?" I ask, touching my newly gifted necklace. I'm also surprised by the little tremble in my voice.

Lukas steps close to me and slides his fingers through my hair. "This is the first time I'm doing something without making plans," he admits. "But I'm more sure about you than I've ever been about anything else."

I release a breath and nod, relaxing into Lukas's chest, my forehead snuggled into the warm crook of his neck. He envelopes me in his arms, and I let myself feel safe.

CHAPTER 24

MY LIFE HAS DONE A COMPLETE ONE-EIGHTY. IN A WAY, IT FEELS LIKE my life has all but stopped in a moment of bliss. This, apparently, is what it's like to stop and smell the roses. Oddly enough, I don't miss Fin-vice at all. It has been strange not seeing my co-workers every day, especially my best bud Thomas, but equally oddly enough, I already feel like I've made a couple of friends here in Maple Falls.

It's been a week since the Autumn Leaves Celebration when Autumn and I made up–that is, when we cleared up some misunderstandings and also confessed our feelings not only to each other, but to ourselves. I've known for a while that I'm all in with Autumn, but as it turned out, she'd been a little reluctant to get attached to a man who was quick to leave. Now, that isn't the case.

I jog down the steps of my apartment that I managed to find and lease at the last second. It's all but empty, but still so much warmer and more inviting than my penthouse back in New York. Autumn helped me buy some new sheets for the bed and insisted on a couple of throw pillows that are amber-colored and velvety textured. I like them because they remind me of her. So does the snake plant sitting by the bay window.

There are still a lot of things to figure out, but some of my arrangements are coming together nicely, and I'm so excited to share these surprises with Autumn.

"Thank you so much," I tell the person on the phone. This is one more arrangement that's going to put the icing on the cake. "I'm really looking forward to this."

I'm about to slip my phone back into my pocket, but I decide I'd better shoot Autumn a text first. I know she's on a tour for another hour, and I haven't talked to her much all day. If I'm lucky, she'll see it and respond soon.

Can I meet you at the tour company after your shift?

My chest feels like it's full of fireworks. I can hardly contain my excitement. For a man who spent the last ten years of his life planning and unknowingly digging himself into a semi-lonely trench, I'm strangely at ease with this whole big life change. I hadn't realized just how much work was weighing me down. And it wasn't just work, but my mindset. I was so focused on success and doing the next thing on the list that I'd really lost sight of the value of daily life, of the small things.

As I drive through town in my rental car, I pass through this town that already feels more like home than New York ever did—the nice, modest houses tucked cozily together, the little shops and restaurants woven in here and there, the cathedral on the edge of town, the winding roads, and the warm hues of amber and gold lingering in the trees. Lots of houses are decked out with Halloween decorations, and already, the youngest little costumed kids out with their parents trick-or-treating before it gets dark.

I pop into the local flower shop that I discovered last week when Autumn and I were taking a stroll. The owner of the place, Mr. Johnson, welcomes me with a friendly smile. I return his kindness and request help with a bouquet. I want something special for Autumn, something that reminds me of her. For a little up charge, Mr. Johnson guides me through building a bouquet. I choose velvety purple peonies and some lighter pinkish colored flowers called Victorian Secret Roses. Mr. Johnson helps me tuck in some greenery pieces and fillers, and I add a single white tulip (I'm told that tulips represent perfect love).

In the next shop over, I grab a card. The woman at the register is jittery with excitement when I tell her that the flowers are for my girlfriend. "Oh, my goodness!" she squeals. "I've seen you two walking around together lately. I've honestly been so curious about your sudden appearance because I knew you weren't from around here."

I smile at the unexpected attention. I guess that's an aspect of being in a small town that I'll have to get used to again. Everyone knows everyone.

The woman at the register, Samantha, her name tag says, sighs dreamily. "I'm so excited she finally found someone. That girl is a treasure."

I wonder how these two know each other. They seem like they could be around the same age, so maybe they went to school or together or something. I make a mental note to mention this interaction to Autumn. I want to know everything about her, hear all of her stories.

"Yes," I reply. "She really is."

An hour later, I arrive at the tour company. Mr. Seeley quickly finds me. I've gotten to know him, too, this last week. I really like the man, and I'm happy that he's been such a supporter of Autumn and her desire to work there. Actually, all the workers seem pretty tight-knit around this place. Mr. Seeley shares some stories with me about Autumn and the twins who work there and their playful bickering. He tells me a few stories about Gus, the bus driver, and how he's been like a grandpa to Autumn. She's told me as much, but I never get tired of hearing about her life here.

Mr. Seeley and I talk shop until the tour bus crunches through the loose gravel and stops nearby. A smattering of people walk off the bus, and I hear Autumn's cheerful voice telling them goodbye and wishing them a good rest of their night. It makes me smile to see her in her element. And I'm not the only one. Mr. Seeley is holding his hands behind his back and watching Autumn with a pleased expression on his face.

My stomach swims. I hope this is the right decision. The right risk.

Autumn spots us standing close by and she jogs over to us, eyeing the bouquet in my hand. A small smile plays at the corner of her mouth like she's waiting for confirmation that she can smile. I want to kiss that curve of her mouth.

"What's going on?" she asks, sliding under my outstretched arm. "Are these for me?"

I nod and hand them over to her. "They sure are."

She takes them eagerly and immediately plants her nose in the middle. Her beautiful green eyes sparkle up at me, brightened by the purple that surrounds them.

Autumn glances between me and Mr. Seeley, sensing there is more to the story. "What's the occasion?" she asks nervously.

I realize then that I was so caught up making the plans that I never decided how to tell Autumn. My mind is trilling, blank.

Thankfully, Mr. Seeley takes a soft step forward and plants a hand on Autumn's shoulder. "You know I've been planning to retire for a while now," he tells her. "And I don't have anyone to take this place over for me, so I've been trying to sell it."

Autumn's smile has softened to barely there, and her eyebrows are slowly drawing together.

"Well," Mr. Seeley continues, glancing at me and clearing his throat. "I finally found a buyer."

Autumn's eyebrows pinch together, and she looks at me then back at Mr. Seeley. He just smiles at her, and she looks at me again. "I don't get it."

"I bought it," I blurt out. "I'm the buyer."

Autumn's green eyes widen, and the bouquet drops slightly. "What?"

"Mr. Seeley was gracious enough to sell the tour company... to me," I say.

All the color drains from Autumn's face, and with it goes a fair amount of the confidence I was secretly clinging onto. I knew this was big, and I really wasn't sure how she was going to take it, but…

"W–why did you do that?" she asks.

I clear my throat, regretting again that I hadn't organized a speech of some kind. "I… want to help you achieve your dreams," I say.

Autumn stares at me, her lips slightly parted, her eyes as big as saucers. "That's… too much. How can you…." She trails off. "I mean, it can't have been cheap, and now…. how do I…?"

I place my hands on either shoulder and crane my head down a little to look into her eyes. "I know it's big, and it's surprising… but I don't want you to worry about the expense."

She blinks at me. Mr. Seeley seems to be biting back a laugh, which isn't exactly encouraging. But I wouldn't have done this if I hadn't known about their close relationship. I made sure to get his opinion—as well as Beverly's—before making this move.

I chuckle lightly and forage ahead. "As I mentioned before, I didn't do much outside of work, and that includes spending money. Even after my parents kept refusing to take any from me, I didn't work any less… and I didn't spend any more. So… I've built quite a bit of savings, and since it's in a high yield account, it sort of snowballed on its own, so… I bought it."

"But what about everything else you'll have to pay for? You'll want to buy a car here, right? And you're not even working right now. Right?"

The concerned look in her eyes makes me smile again. "I'm working on that," I reassure her. "I have an interview with a financial services company in Grant. But even if I don't get the job, I still have enough funds to take a few years off work."

Her eyes widen again. "A few years?! Even after buying an entire company?"

I brush my finger over Autumn's cheek, which is slowly gaining some color back. She's searching my face, maybe looking for some sign of jest. "I worked too many hours, remember?" I mutter. Then I add, "But I think this is what I've been working toward. Autumn, I know you'll grow this place and make it your own, and I really want to see you do something you've always wanted."

Her color is gone again. The flowers remain in her hand but fall limp with her arm. "Me?"

Mr. Seeley peers giddily at Autumn and nods. "I'm so excited to leave this place in your hands. As I might have mentioned before, I think it's time you take on a higher role."

With a shuddering breath, Autumn sucks in the cool evening air. That's when I notice her eyes welling up. I gently brush away the tears that fall with my hooked finger.

"Now, I can finally retire and spend more time with Margie," Mr. Seeley adds.

"Lukas," Autumn cried softly. "This is…. How do I… pay you back? I don't have anything—"

"Autumn," I say firmly but with a smile curving up. "This is a gift. If you don't want it, that's fine; just say the word. And if you do accept, then how about you pay me back is by letting me see the joy in you, you here in your element, where you belong, showing all these people what you love about Maple Falls."

Her lips are trembling a little, but I can see the light returning to her face.

"I'll let you two talk it over," Mr. Seeley says, bowing his head before stepping away. His slow steps crunch on the gravel.

"Can you handle more news?" I tease her.

She groans in exasperation. "More?"

I chuckle and resist planting a kiss on those perfect heart-shaped lips right then and there. "I found a house, you know, a more permanent place than an apartment. And I want you to check it out with me."

She is simply incredulous, her eyes getting wider. I stroke her neck lightly with my fingertips, feeling her pulse pumping quickly.

"I don't want to overwhelm you any more than I already have," I say. "But maybe someday, you know, in the future, you can help me turn it into a home?"

A couple of tears spill over, and I wipe them away with my thumbs. She is so precious. I want to give her everything.

"Really?" she finally squeaks out.

That's all it takes to split my face into a crazy big grin. I nod and tuck her hair behind her ear. "I know it's early, and I don't want to rush you, but I can say with confidence that this is what I want. You are what I want."

"So you're buying a house?" she asks.

I nod.

"And you're getting a job… here?"

I nod again.

"You're staying here… permanently?" she whispers like if she says it too loud, I'll wake up and change my mind.

I chuckle and nod once more.

After a couple of seconds she adds, "And you bought this company?" She points to the building beside us. "For me?"

I nod another time, a sly smile sliding over my face. "To be paid back, remember?"

Finally, Autumn cracks… a smile that is. "Can I make my first payment of joy now?" she asks timidly.

My pulse quickens. I nod one more time and lean down. My hands find their place, one at the small of Autumn's back and the other cupping her lovely face. She closes her eyes and presses off her toes to meet my lips.

CHAPTER 25

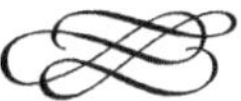

I've never considered myself the cheerleader type, but watching Lukas find his element on this volleyball team has morphed me into the proud, face-painted girlfriend yelling from the sidelines as Lukas dives into the hardwood floor, digging a hard spike and keeping the ball live.

"Yeah!" I scream, hopping up and down. "Way to go, babe!"

At first I think he's too in the zone to hear me, but once he's up on his feet again, he finds me and sends a wink my way. Aunt Bev knocks her shoulder into me playfully. "You two are so cute, it's gross. I love it."

I laugh, blushing a little. "Me, too."

It's so obvious that Lukas is happy here. A year ago, when I first laid eyes on him, he was stunning, but he was stern-looking and serious. Over the following month—let's be real, it… was within the first week of knowing him—I fell for his charm and his surprising down-to-earth demeanor. Somehow, magically, we fit together, and despite my fears and his unawakened desire to actually live life, we were able to come together and find a space for love.

And, oh, how I love this man.

I love when he kisses me goodnight. I love seeing his car pull up after work. I love taking walks with him and Tess. I love baseball games with him and Aunt Bev. I love how he encourages me when I face a new challenge at the tour company. I love how his face glows when he plays volleyball with his new friends. I love how he smiles crookedly when his parents try to FaceTime him. And I love the way he looks at me. I love the way he loves me, too.

The last year has been nothing short of magical. Mr. Seeley stuck around for a few months to help me get some management experience under my belt, but I've been running the company by myself since June, and while summer was tough, I feel stronger after that experience, and I'm thrilled to be tackling my first fall season on my own—well on my own plus a very gracious staff and a very supportive family and boyfriend.

When the volleyball game is over, Lukas runs over to me. His skin is slick from sweat and his face is flushed from exertion, but I don't mind. He steals a quick kiss and threatens to hug Aunt Bev. She hunkers down like she's about to fight off a bear. When he backs down, she ruffles his hair instead, quickly retracting her hand with a loud, "Ugh!" and shaking off his sweat.

We all share a laugh. I seriously wonder if I could ever be happier than I am right now.

"You better shower, boy," Aunt Bev threatens. "Ain't no way I can handle this drench and stench all night. And I'm afraid even the scent of caramel covered apples and funnel cakes won't mask it."

"Of course, he'll take a shower," I say. "It's an important night!"

It's our one-year anniversary. At least, it's what we like to call our anniversary. Lukas wanted to call our first date our anniversary date, but I said it would make more sense if it was the day he told me he was going to stay in Maple Falls. He eventually agreed, though sometimes he still argues that we should use the day we ran into each other in the woods outside the inn because that's when he fell for me.

"I want to look and smell my best," Lukas says, circling his arm around my waist. "For tonight's surprise."

I roll my eyes; then register what he said. "Wait," I say, planting a hand on his sturdy chest. "What surprise?"

Lukas bats his eyelashes at me innocently and shrugs one shoulder.

Something has been nagging me all night. Lukas and I went to the Kissing Bridge and had a cute late picnic lunch after his volleyball game this morning. Now we've arrived at the Autumn Leaves Celebration. It's our first anniversary as a couple, and it seems like Lukas is aware of something that I'm not. Since earlier, he's been going on about some surprise. It has me a little on edge and a little curious.

Right now we're walking through the middle of the Autumn Leaves Celebration. The air is warmer than last year, but we still walk hand in hand in his jacket pocket. It's become our thing, I guess. We've just met Cally for lunch and are on the way to check on Aunt Bev's store. Now that I'm working full time at the tour company, I haven't been helping her as often. She hired a new girl named Olive, who just graduated high school this year.

Lukas and I stroll up to the window and peek in. Blue Kiss is busy, but it looks like everything is moving like a well-oiled machine. Olive is at the register with a friendly customer-service smile plastered on her face and her red hair tied back in a long ponytail. Even from here, I can see a drop of sweat on her temple. Poor girl. Meanwhile, my Aunt Beverly is flitting around the store, showing items to customers and occasionally tidying up the shelves.

"Should we go in?" Lukas asks.

I shake my head. "Not right now. It looks like they have everything under control."

Lukas gives my hand a squeeze. Before we step away, Aunt Bev catches sight of us in the window and gives us a wink. Strange, I think. I never knew her to be much of a winker. Then again... I look up at the strapping man standing next to me, my boyfriend. Who wouldn't feel the urge to wink at him?

"What?" Lukas asks, a suspicious crook in his smile.

I poke him in the faint smile line with my free hand. "Just feeling lucky to have you. That's all."

Lukas grabs my hand with his free hand and pulls it to his chest. "Can't be any luckier than I am," he says, planting a soft peck on my nose.

My tummy swirls, touched by the sweet gesture and yet wanting a little more.

We take off down the street again. "So, about this surprise you've been going on about all day," I begin. "Are you going to tell me anything else about it?"

A gentle breeze gusts through, sweeping Lukas's moppy brown hair across his forehead. He's grown it out over the last year, and I like the way it gives him a little boyish charm. Although I'm not one to complain about his old hairstyle, this laid-back version feels truer to his personality.

"Are you ready to see it now?" he asks. He glances at his watch and grins over at me. "Now should be good."

The way he's looking at me makes my heart somersault. I haven't seen him this excited since he told me he bought the tour company. The lights are on behind his dark brown eyes, begging me to follow suit with his mystery plan. How can I say no to him when he's like this?

Lukas picks up the pace a little, towing me close beside him. I let out a girlish giggle as his urgency pulls us through the crowd. Everything is the same beautiful fall theme as every other year. I recognize the same faces plus a few new ones, and the same tents and booths. Very little has changed in my life here, except for the very prominent difference that is Lukas. And though I've loved this town to my core, it feels brighter now that he's in it.

I've been lost in thought, staring at the side of the love of my life's face, and a couple quick minutes later we screech to a halt in the middle of the town square. Lukas glances down and finally meets my eyes. He has curled in his lips to combat an expressive smile.

"Are you ready?" he asks.

My eyes are locked on his, searching for… something… until he gestures beside us.

We're standing in the middle of the town square, except erected here on the edge is a beautiful mahogany gazebo surrounded by a swarm of string lights. All around the gazebo are vases of flowers, and red and orange leafed garlands. In front of the steps are several small gourds and pumpkins in the shape of a heart. Inside the gazebo is a little podium with a lantern on it.

My heart sinks in the best way, as if a marshmallow melting into the warmth of hot cocoa. "What is this?" I whisper.

Lukas takes our hands out of his pocket and guides us inside the gazebo. Every step is slow and measured as he settles me beside the little podium. Upon closer examination, I see a little layout of photos of us, little snapshots of our last year together. Each one is dated in the corner with his sprawling handwriting. A gradual smile teases the corner of my mouth.

"Lukas…" I whisper. "This is so nice."

As I'm reaching out to touch the photographs, Lukas stoops down. No… he kneels.

Wait. He kneels?!

My smile falls as my brain shoots flares on red alert. He's kneeling! As in on one knee! And he's holding my hand! And he's looking at me with a serious kind of hope in his eyes.

"Autumn," he whispers. His voice soothes my mind just enough, but now it's like it's locked on a target. I watch as he reaches with his left hand into his pocket and pulls out a small red velvet-coated box.

That was in there the whole time….

"Autumn," he says again. This time I register the slight shake in his voice. Lukas is rubbing his right hand over my knuckles, and in the left he's gripping what most certainly is a box with a ring in it. "Every day, you remind me what a blessing life is. Before I met you, I was living inside myself, working literally hundred hour weeks sometimes, just checking off the boxes for success… but when I got dragged here, to Maple Falls, and I met you, it became clear to me just how much of life I had checked out of."

My mouth is desert dry. I wet my lips and wait with bated breath.

"But you wore through the jaded parts of me with every laugh, every explained detail of how the leaves change and how the geese migrate. You brighten my life a little more every time you look at me. I love you, and I love that you've helped me grow into someone I never knew I wanted to be, someone who loves life and has fun." He scrunches his nose up a little, and it makes me crack a smile.

Oh, my heart….

"Autumn," he says for the third time. He releases my hand and opens the little red box to reveal a simple golden ring with an inset diamond and a beautiful, intricate leaf pattern etched into the band. With my hands free, I don't know what to do but reach out for Lukas's hand again.

He gives a little laugh and reaches back out for me, letting me envelop his hand with both of mine for a little while longer, to steady me. I realize that a quiver is dancing through my body.

"This last year has easily been the greatest of my life, and I have no doubt that the best years are yet to come as long as I get to spend them with you. So, selfishly, I want to start that time now, with you. And I promise that I will strive every day to be the man that you deserve. I promise I will cherish you, and I will love and support you. I will grow with you, I will settle with you, I will fall in love with you over and over again. So please, Autumn, please join me in this journey for the rest of our lives…. Will you be my wife?"

I collapse into a crouch and throw my arms around Lukas. Thank God for his strong legs. He's able to support my weight without us toppling over.

"I had no idea you were planning this," I cry into the crook of his neck.

A low chuckle rumbles up, shaking in his throat and tickling the skin on my face. "I gave you a hint."

I pull back slightly, and Lukas supports me. "When?"

He hands the ring box off to his other hand that's cupped against the small of my back and uses his other hand to wipe my face. Silent tears have begun to streak down, but I didn't even realize it. "When we went to look at the house I bought. Remember? I told you I wanted you to help me make it a home."

The tears are fierce now because I've never been so happy. I've never felt so loved as I have now on the cold wooden floor of this glowing gazebo in the middle of the Autumn Leaves Celebration. "That was a year ago!" I cried, gathering as much of the man in front of me as I can hold in my arms.

Lukas wraps his other arm around me and squeezes me so tight I stop crying. "I know," he whispers into my hair.

I sniffle and brave another look at him. His eyes, too, are brimming with tears. It's my turn this time to dab them away. I use the cuff of my sweater. "What took you so long, then?" I mutter.

He cracks a grin. "Are you mad?"

I nod, but I'm smiling, albeit a little sheepishly.

"And I can put this ring on your finger?" Lukas asks.

My head rocks back and forth.

The ring fits perfectly, and it suits me just right. It's simple and delicate. I inspect it closely just for a second before taking Lukas's face in my hands. "I love you so much," I say, pulling him toward me. He closes the distance between us easily, bracing my back with his muscular arms and meeting my lips with tender urgency. We share a long, deep kiss that ignites my insides.

"How about a fall wedding?" Lukas mutters breathlessly against my mouth.

I grin and kiss him again.

Thank you for reading! Cally's story is now available. Read chapter 1 now and find Cold Turkey *here.*

COLD TURKEY CHAPTER 1

THE FRAGRANT ONIONS SIZZLE IN THE PAN, MAKING MY MOUTH WATER. My stomach gurgles in annoyance. I give it a gentle pat and say, "Just fifteen more minutes," reaching through the industrial-sized refrigerator door and grabbing another pound of hamburger and some lettuce, ignoring my fussy tummy until my lunch break.

My parents' restaurant, Maple Falls Café, has been very busy today. I've been assisting in the kitchen, bustling around getting the orders cooked, plated, and to the serving window, while secretly adding a little extra pizzazz to a dish once in a while.

It's not that the food is bad, but I like to have fun with it, and while I'm working here, I'm limited to my parents' recipes. Most of my cooking is done after hours or in my kitchen, and there, I have the freedom to experiment.

"Cally Stein, you know we don't put cilantro in that," my dad cautions me from the stove.

I yank my hand back from the soup cup I'm about to put in the serving window and spin around, shoving the cilantro down into the front of my apron pocket. "What cilantro?" I try to say innocently.

My dad suppresses a laugh and shakes his head. "Sweetie, I know you think your versions are better, and I'll admit that you've got good taste, but people don't want to be surprised here," he says in his soulful voice. "My recipes haven't changed in ten years, hun. Changing things now could break the town's trust."

My shoulders slump. I know it's the truth. Maple Falls Café is known for its dependable taste and familiar menu. My dad is the main cook, and he's kind but strict when it comes to following his recipes. I've been helping him since I was fifteen and know how to make every item on the menu by heart. But I really enjoy cooking, and I want to share some of my creations once in a while.

I roll my shoulders and strengthen my resolve. "What about the seasonal dish menu we talked about? Have you thought about it? I can make some samples for you. I have a lot of good ideas—"

My dad raises his hand and turns back to his soup pot. "We'll talk about it later," he says. "Let's get through this rush first."

I peek through the serving window and note that almost every single booth and table is full. I'm amazed that my dad can do all this cooking by himself most days, since our other cooks are part time. I've been pretty much full time since getting my culinary degree, but we don't always work the same shift.

Jarred and Andrea, our servers, zip through their sections, topping off drinks and passing out receipts. My mother, Cara, is manning the register, seating new customers, and handling the cashiering. Mom is the face of Maple Falls Café. The place was born of my father's desire, but my mom keeps it afloat. And I… do what I can here and there and try to help.

Fifteen minutes turn into thirty when a group of ten teachers comes in. Several of them look the same as they did when I left high school eight years ago. One of my former classmates is actually among them—Jen. This must be her second year teaching high school. Why she wanted to return there is a million-dollar question to me. I remember how excited we all were to graduate and spend our days somewhere else, finally.

When I finally get to take a quick break, I hang my patchwork apron on a hook on the wall by the swinging door and meet my mom behind the register. She's just finished ringing up the recently retired Maple Falls Tour Company owner, Mr. Randal Seeley, and his wife, Margie. I wave hello before they leave, and Mr. Seeley shares his signature radiant smile.

"You doing okay?" I ask my mom, moving her long black ponytail off her shoulder so it hangs down her back. I note the little beads of sweat on the nape of her neck.

"I'm good, sweetie," she says, rubbing a couple of quick circles on my back. "You taking a break?"

I look out at the bustling restaurant, the large group of teachers seated in the middle. Several of the tables look close to finishing.

"Nah," I say. "I came to relieve you for a bit. Dad, uh, wants your opinion on something in the back. Something about a supply order, maybe?"

My mother squints at me, but it seems like she's taking my word for it, so I place my hands on her shoulders and guide her toward the back.

"Yeah, yeah," I continue. "It was definitely about the next supply order. Feel free to take your time, and I'll take over here for a little bit."

My mother sighs. "I don't know why this couldn't wait until later," she grumbles.

Since I've managed to trick my mother into taking a break, I do my part, ringing up the group of teachers and a couple of other tables who have finished their food. When she returns about twenty minutes later, I go back to helping my father in the kitchen until we close.

Dad lets me fix the three of us a late dinner in the cafe kitchen. Since our restaurant is more of a diner than a fancy restaurant, there are limited ingredients. I manage to whip together a recipe I have been trying to get my dad to add as a specialty or seasonal item: loaded chili dogs, with Amoroso rolls split at the top and slightly hollowed out to accommodate more filling, smoky-flavored grilled hotdogs, and sweet chili topped with salty crushed corn nuts and spicy jalapeños. For a personalized taste, I prepare some cucumber radish and sour cream.

I wanted to come up with a cute name for them, but I'd given up after my dad turned down my last couple of ideas. What can I say? He's a man of tradition. He knows what has worked for him so far, and he doesn't want to "mess up perfection," as he puts it.

While I'm cooking, my parents get started on redecorating the restaurant, taking down the skeletons, jack-o'-lanterns, and black felt cats. Halloween is over now, and, as always, it was a lot of fun!

I was happy to see Meena, my cousin, dress up as her favorite video game character Ha-nana, since last year she bailed on that idea and opted to be a princess like her friends. It seems like she's slowly becoming her own person and letting that shine. I'm happy for her. My quirky little wind-up doll costume totally slayed. But as much as I enjoy Halloween, Thanksgiving gives me life–the food is its crowning glory!

We eat the loaded chili dogs as a family in one of the booths, making small talk about my older siblings, who have all moved on and left this restaurant and town behind.

My mother makes a couple of comments about how tasty the dinner is, and my dad simply nods in agreement. After eating our fill, we dedicate the next two hours to decking out the restaurant with little golden turkeys and cornucopias, leaves and acorns, and various squashes and gourds.

By the end of it, my mind is swirling with ideas for new recipes to try for our family meal. It's only a few weeks away!

It's slow the next night, so I'm able to take a long dinner break when my best friend Autumn and her fiancé Lukas swing by the restaurant for dinner. I have to admit that I was very surprised at first that the two of them got together. I didn't know Lukas before because he is from out of town, but it was clear early on how smitten Autumn was with him.

Things were great with them at first—until she disassociated because he said he was going to move back to New York. But then he didn't, and he bought the tour company where she worked and gave it to her! It was a whole whirlwind affair if I've ever seen one!

But now, seeing them together over the last year, watching both of them come out of their shells and challenge each other and also comfort each other–man, that's what dreams are made of. My dreams, anyway....

"Wow! It's like fall threw up in here. I love it!" Autumn says. I know it's her way of praising the decor.

"Sweetheart, look." Lukas points out the waterfall of string lights in the bar area.

It's so sweet the way Autumn immediately turns to see what he's pointing at. Her green eyes take on a lovely glow as she studies the setup at the bar, with string lights and tendrils of leaves and pinecones. "Reminds me of the little gazebo in the middle of the fall festival where we got engaged," she croons, wrinkling her nose at him adorably.

He takes her hand and kisses the beautiful golden ring on her finger. It's so sweet, my stomach cinches up. I hope they will be this cute and happy forever.

And I hope I'm lucky enough to find a nice guy who loves me like that, one I can share my life with.

My heart aches a little, but I breathe out the pinching sensation with a puff of air and focus on my friends. "How's the wedding planning going?" I ask as we slide into a corner booth, with them on one side and me on the other.

They share a guilty look. "We haven't even started planning," they say simultaneously. Autumn shrugs her coat off her shoulders, and Lukas kindly folds it neatly beside him.

Ugh. I hate how much love these people right now. As a single girl, it's hard sometimes to be around them.

"Well, I hope you've at least decided who your maid of honor will be!" I tease.

Between Autumn owning and operating Maple Falls Tour Company and getting engaged, I haven't seen her much lately. We used to get together three or four times a week, and now it feels like it's three entire weeks since I've seen her. Plus, I love Lukas, too, but he's always here now. It might not be so bad if I had a guy of my own so we could double date, but I don't have anyone like that.

And not a single prospect.

We eat and chat for a couple of hours before Autumn tells me she's got to get to bed so she can wake up early to oversee a large group of tourists first thing in the morning. Lukas admits that he's exhausted from his earlier volleyball game and that he's ready to hit the hay, too. So, we wrap it up and say goodbye, parting ways like we don't know when we'll see each other again.

Since the cafe is still basically empty, my parents send me home. I start out on my walk home—four blocks south and another six blocks east to the little two-bedroom house I rent. The air is quiet and cold, and the sky is overcast with dimly moonlit clouds. T

he calm has my mind wandering. It suddenly strikes me how alone I feel without Autumn and without my parents. Even my other bestie, Ivy Dear, is working overtime at Hearthlight Inn, the bed and breakfast inn her parents own, with peak vacation season encroaching.

Everyone loves the fall colors in Maple Falls—especially the tourists.

My thoughts drift back to Autumn and Lukas. They're such a star couple. But as wonderful as it would be to have a charming man of my own, it's hard to imagine. I know every single man in this town, and everybody of marriageable age is already in a relationship, or they're just totally not my type.

Also, what even is my type? Maybe I haven't met anyone who fits it yet because I've always just been here. Maybe the only hope of me finding my other half is... leaving?

I gulp at the thought. I love Maple Falls. There's nowhere else I'd want to live.

Maybe I'll get lucky and have the perfect guy just show up here one day, just like what happened for Autumn.

A girl can dream.

*K*EEP *R*EADING! *F*IND *C*OLD *T*URKEY *HERE!*

ALSO BY ID JOHNSON

Stand Alone Titles

<u>All I Want for Christmas is Pooch</u>

(*sweet contemporary romance*)

<u>Christmas Memory</u>

(*sweet contemporary romance*)

<u>Meet Cute Me Under the Mistletoe</u>

(*sweet contemporary romance*)

<u>The Doll Maker's Daughter at Christmas</u>

(*clean romance/historical*)

<u>Pretty Little Monster</u>

(*young adult/suspense*)

<u>The Journey to Normal: Our Family's Life with Autism</u> (*nonfiction*)

<u>Found by the Alpha (*fantasy romance*)</u>

Sweet As Maple Syrup series

Leaving Autumn

Cold Turkey (coming Nov 1, 2025!)

Snowed Inn (coming Dec 1, 2025!)

Love Throughout Time

(*time travel romance*)

Back to Titanic

Back to Gettysburg

Back to Bunker Hill

Back to the Highlands

Back to Port Royal

Back to the Inquisition

Back to Salem (Oct 2025)

Back to Plymouth (Nov 2025)

Back to Whitechapel (Dec 2025)

Back to the Old West (Jan 2026)

Back to the Ton (Feb 2026)

Back to the Crown (March 2026)

Back to Pompeii (April 2026)

Silverwood Academy

(paranormal romance)

Vampire Hunter

World Builder

Realm Jumper

Celestial Springs

(psychological thriller/literary fiction/women's fiction)

Beneath the Inconstant Moon

The First Mrs. Edwards

Leaving Ginny

The Motherhood

(dystopian romance)

Rain's Rebellion

Rain's Run

Rain's Return

Ashes and Rose Petals

(contemporary romance/retelling of Romeo and Juliet and Cinderella)

Girl in the Attic

Girl From the Tomb

<u>Girl On the Beach</u>

Nashville Country Dreams

(contemporary romance)

<u>Meant to Marry Me</u>

<u>Lead Me Home</u>

<u>You Are the Reason</u>

Forever Love series

(clean romance/historical)

<u>Cordia's Will: A Civil War Story of Love and Loss</u>

<u>Cordia's Hope: A Story of Love on the Frontier</u>

The Clandestine Saga series

(paranormal romance)

<u>Transformation</u>

<u>Resurrection</u>

<u>Repercussion</u>

<u>Absolution</u>

<u>Illumination</u>

<u>Destruction</u>

<u>Annihilation</u>

<u>Obliteration</u>

<u>Termination</u>

A Vampire Hunter's Tale (based on The Clandestine Saga)

(paranormal/alternate history)

<u>Aaron</u>

<u>Jamie</u>

<u>Elliott</u>

<u>Christian</u>

The Chronicles of Cassidy (based on The Clandestine Saga)

(young adult paranormal)

<u>So You Think Your Sister's a Vampire Hunter?</u>

<u>Who Wants to Be a Vampire Hunter?</u>

<u>How Not to Be a Vampire Hunter</u>

<u>My Life As a Teenage Vampire Hunter</u>

<u>Vampire Hunting Isn't for Morons</u>

<u>Vampires Bite and Other Life Lessons</u>

<u>Gone Guardian</u>

<u>Death Does Not Become Her</u>

Blood of the Vampire Hunter (based on The Clandestine Saga)

(paranormal romance)

<u>Night Slayer</u>

<u>Shadow Stalker</u>

<u>Queen Catcher</u>

<u>Mother Hunter</u>

<u>Father Finder</u>

Ghosts of Southampton series

(historical romance)

<u>Prelude</u>

<u>Titanic</u>

<u>Residuum</u>

<u>Lusitania</u>

Heartwarming Holidays Sweet Romance series

(Christian/clean romance)

<u>Melody's Christmas</u>

<u>Christmas Cocoa</u>

<u>Winter Woods</u>

<u>Waiting On Love</u>

<u>Shamrock Hearts</u>

<u>A Blossoming Spring Romance</u>

<u>Firecracker!</u>

<u>Falling in Love</u>

<u>Thankful for You</u>

<u>Melody's Christmas Wedding</u>

<u>The New Year's Date</u>

Charles Town Brides (based on Heartwarming Holidays Sweet Romance)

(Christian/clean romance)

<u>From This Moment</u>

<u>Can't Help Falling in Love</u>

<u>It's Your Love</u>

<u>When You Say Nothing At All</u>

<u>My Girl</u>

<u>Unchained Melody</u>

<u>I Only Have Eyes For You</u>

<u>At Last</u>

<u>The Very Thought of You</u>

Reaper's Hollow

(paranormal/urban fantasy)

<u>Ruin's Lot</u>

<u>Ruin's Promise</u>

<u>Ruin's Legacy</u>

When Kings Collide

(steamy historical romance)

<u>Princess of Silence</u>

<u>Princess of Hearts</u>

Collections

<u>Ghosts of Southampton Books 0-2</u>

<u>Reaper's Hollow Books 1-3</u>

<u>The Clandestine Saga Books 1-3</u>

<u>The Chronicles of Cassidy Books 1-4</u>

<u>Celestial Springs Collection</u>

<u>Heartwarming Holidays Sweet Romance Books 1-3</u>

<u>Heartwarming Holidays Sweet Romance Books 4-7</u>

Websites: https://idjohnsonwriter.com/

Follow us on TikTok: @roguewolfpublishing

Follow on Twitter @authoridjohnson

Find me on Facebook at <u>www.facebook.com/IDJohnsonAuthor</u>

Instagram: @authoridjohnson

Follow me on Bookbub: https://www.bookbub.com/authors/id-johnson